new town soul

New Town Soul was written by the author as part of Dún Laoghaire-Rathdown County Council's 'Place and Identity' Programme of Per Cent for Art commissions for 2008-2010 funded through the Department of the Environment, Heritage and Local Government

Novels

Night Shift
The Woman's Daughter
The Journey Home
Emily's Shoes
A Second Life
Father's Music
Temptation
The Valparaiso Voyage
The Family on Paradise Pier

Collaborative Novels

*Finbar's Hotel**
*Ladies Night at Finbar's Hotel**

Plays

The Lament for Arthur Cleary
Blinded by the Light
*In High Germany**
The Holy Ground
One Last White Horse
April Bright
*The Passion of Jerome**
Consenting Adults
*From These Green Heights***
*The Townlands of Brazil***
*Walking the Road**
*The Consequences of Lightning***
The Parting Glass

Poetry

The Habit of Flesh
Finglas Lilies
No Waiting America
Internal Exiles
Leinster Street Ghosts
Taking My Letters Back
The Chosen Moment
*External Affairs**

Editor

The Picador Book of Contemporary Irish Fiction (UK)
The Vintage Book of Contemporary Irish Fiction (USA)
Night & Day: Twenty Four Hours in the Life of Dublin

(*Available from New Island
**Available from New Island under the title *The Ballymun Trilogy*)

new town soul

DERMOT BOLGER

Little Island

First published 2010
by Little Island
an imprint of New Island
2 Brookside
Dundrum Road
Dublin 14

www.littleisland.ie

ISBN 978-1-84840-946-0

British Library Cataloguing Data. A CIP catalogue record for this book is available from the British Library.

Book design by Inka Hagen

Printed in Ireland by ColourBooks.

J272.534 €9.00

Little Island received financial assistance from
The Arts Council (An Chomhairle Ealaíon), Dublin, Ireland.

arts council / chomhairle ealaíon
funding literature
artscouncil.ie

10 9 8 7 6 5 4 3 2 1

For my sister, Deirdre, with love

ONE

Thomas

1932

The music of a jazz record on the gramophone fills the doctor's study. Thomas tries not to listen to the music as he feels the cold stethoscope against his skin, but the saxophone solo overwhelms him, conjuring up images of foreign cities and adventure.

Old Dr Thomson removes the stethoscope and stares at the boy's anxious face.

'No need to look scared, Thomas. With a heart like yours, you'll live forever.'

'Fr O'Connor says that jazz is the devil's music; it can inflame terrible passions and steal your soul.'

The doctor laughs. He crosses the book-lined study to raise the volume of the music.

'How can any type of music be bad, child? Souls can be stolen, but not by something as innocent as jazz.'

'How then?'

The doctor turns, his eyes serious. 'Have you ever heard of a changeling?'

'No.'

'Some mothers believe that dark spirits can steal their babies while they sleep and replace them in the cot with malevolent beings who are neither truly alive nor truly dead. Changelings.'

'Do you believe in changelings, doctor?'

The old man shrugs. 'I've been a doctor for fifty years. My family were doctors here in Blackrock for five generations before me. Two hundred years ago my grandfather's grandfather was called to the Hellfire Club. A young servant boy had found his master with his throat cut. The man was notorious in Blackrock. He was the last of the Dawson family – you know, the people who owned Castledawson House. He was a rake. He'd gambled his way through a fortune and was in the final throes of consumption, unable to stop coughing blood. Do you know the Hellfire Club?'

'No.'

'It's a burned-out ruin now. You can still see what's left of it in the Dublin hills. It was used by rakes who drank in the notorious Eagle Tavern in Dublin. People say Dawson had grown sick of it: toasting the devil's health with raw whiskey mixed with melted butter in front of a blazing fire, until the merciless heat and alcohol made the drinker pass out. Whole estates were gambled away there yet he couldn't stop himself being lured up there to the games of cards and dice that were played amid oaths and blasphemy and the constant invocations for the dark lord – Beelzebub, Lucifer – to appear in the guise of a black cat.

'Nobody would gamble with Dawson any more, because he had nothing left to bet with, but some say that he had one final wager with the devil. No one knows what happened on that morning when Michael Byrne, his servant boy, came to collect him up at the club, but old folk in Blackrock claimed that Dawson made one final wish and tricked Michael Byrne into making a wish too. They used the relics of a saint to make their wish, fragments of bone that had been in Dawson's family for generations. It was believed that those relics had the power to grant one's most fervent wishes. But desire has a dark side; no wish comes without a price. They say that Michael Byrne later had those bones carved into the shape of gambling dice. If Byrne wished for gold, he got his wish, because he had the devil's own luck with cards and dice ever after. No one knows what Henry Dawson wished for, because Michael Byrne always claimed that when he found his master, Dawson's throat had already been cut with a black-handled knife.'

'Did Byrne do it?' asks Thomas. 'Murder his master?'

'Some folk claimed he did. Others said that Byrne had become a changeling when he returned to Blackrock after that day; because there was something about him utterly different from the starving servant boy who had set out to fetch his master. I still have my grandfather's grandfather's medical notes about the case. He considered that the boy had become mentally unhinged at finding the body. If he had somehow become a changeling, it was not in the way that peasants mean. My great-great-grandfather wondered if the boy's soul had been snatched in some way. It seemed to him as if other beings were lodged inside his body, dead souls gazing out through the boy's bewildered eyes. Does that make sense to you, Thomas?'

'No.'

The doctor smiles. 'And you are undoubtedly right, Thomas; such stories are myth and superstition. All I can say for certain is that jazz will not harm you. Still, whatever you do in life, never let anyone snatch your soul.'

The record ends. Thomas hears the soft *putt, putt* of the needle as the disc keeps revolving amid a hissing silence.

'How could anyone snatch my soul?'

'By making a pact with you; by promising you your heart's most hidden desire. What do you desire most, Thomas?'

The boy rises and lovingly examines the foreign place names printed in gold leaf on the doctor's radiogram next to the gramophone: Cairo and Hilversum, Helsinki and Paris, Berlin and Copenhagen. He is mesmerised by the thought that if he turns off the record and twists this dial, then indistinct voices from across the world would fill the room like ghosts whispering. Thomas does not want to express his overwhelming desire to travel the world, because he will never be free to do as he wishes. Turning away he notices a carved wooden doll on the sideboard.

'Open it,' the old doctor says.

'What do you mean?'

Dr Thomson picks up the wooden doll to reveal how it comes apart in the middle. Inside the first doll there is another doll, slightly smaller but an exact replica.

'I bought this from an émigré in Paris,' the doctor says, 'a White Russian fleeing the Bolsheviks. In Russia these are called *matryoschka* or nesting dolls.'

The doctor reveals a succession of other carved dolls inside the first one, each one fitting inside the previous one, until twelve of them are lined up along the sideboard.

'They're beautiful,' Thomas says.

The doctor nods. 'But oddly cruel. Imagine what it must feel like to be a doll within a doll, to lose your own identity and spend your life in darkness sandwiched between replicas of yourself, knowing that another face has been placed over yours. Thankfully dolls do not need to breathe, because these dolls would suffocate.' The doctor begins to fit them back inside each other. 'I suspect this is what my grandfather's grandfather meant by being a changeling, someone forced to be part of a chain after some person or power has snatched their soul. Addiction, compulsion, desired – these are all forms of slavery. Go home, Thomas. Tell your mother your chest is fine. But take this record as my present.'

'Fr O'Connor wouldn't like me owning a jazz record. He says I'm going to be a priest.'

'Life rarely works out as we expect, Thomas. You don't know what you will be. But whatever dangers lie ahead for you, they will not come from jazz music. Keep your soul safe, Thomas; because once it is stolen it can never truly be your own again.'

TWO

Joey's Father

1993

Music pounds from the speakers in my dad's speeding car. Not the mindless throb of synthesisers or the robotic vocals of smart blondes managed by dumb men, but a rough cut of tracks from his long-anticipated debut album. Those unfinished songs keep him company on his long drive home to us in Blackrock, his mind buzzing with improvements to the lyrics as he speeds around each sharp bend. Night drives are part of any singer's life: routes like this deserted country road across the Dublin mountains. As Dad puts his foot down, the lines of cat's eyes that loom out from the darkness make him feel like he is inside a computer game.

He has just finished gigging in a hotel in a remote Wicklow glen. His amp was barely able to drown out the incessant thump of a karaoke machine in the public bar. Thirty spellbound fans had crowded around him afterwards, demanding to know when his album, *New Town Soul*, would finally be released. *Hot Press* magazine had tipped it to be the hottest debut of the year. But *Hot Press* had been tipping it to be the best debut for the past three years. Different record companies have signed him up and then released him, unable to prise the master tapes from his hands. Dad cannot give fans a definite release date, because he keeps tinkering with arrangements, striving to create the perfect sound that will grant him immortality. He refuses to settle for anything less than a sound which will ensure his voice lives on forever – like Kurt Cobain before he shot himself; like Sam Cooke and Marvin Gaye before others shot them; like Buddy Holly and Richie Valens before they unwisely boarded rickety aeroplanes; like Jimi Hendrix before he asphyxiated on vomit and wine; like Jim Morrison before junk clogged his brains and veins; like Phil Lynott before the laureate of Dublin could barely find a vein on the soles of his feet to inject into; like the other immortals that my dad listened to, convinced that he was destined to be counted among them one day.

When he releases *New Town Soul*, he knows the crowds will be ten times bigger, but tonight it has been enough that a few hardcore fans turned up to hear his masterpiece in progress. It is a dark country road, but Dad has no intention of wasting money we cannot afford on a hotel. He can be parked outside our tiny cottage in a Victorian terrace before dawn. He knows every shortcut from the endless gigs, from the night-time drives home. He is about to pass the ruins of the Hellfire Club where rakes once drank and toasted the devil. Just beyond that there will be a turn for Tibradden. From there a necklace of neon lights will guide him down into Whitechurch and along the Blackglen Road, past Sandyford Industrial Estate and the

N11 and onto Newtownpark Avenue in Blackrock. From there it will be a left turn onto Frascati Road and then Temple Road. He will need to swing onto the main street of Blackrock, with the seafront and the abandoned baths just a few hundred yards away beyond the train tracks. Then he will swing into Brusna Cottages – the small cul-de-sac where my mother waits for him in a king-sized bed so large that it barely leaves space in the cramped bedroom for the cot where I sleep fretfully, getting my first teeth.

However, this is a journey home that he is never to complete. I like to imagine that at two a.m. a faint echo of the crash somehow wakes me. A sound that only a baby can hear: the sound of my future turning upside down. Does Dad take his hand off the wheel to raise the volume? Does he glance up to see something blocking the road as he rounds the bend – a sheep straying off the mountain, an old man in a black hat brandishing a raised stick or the ghost of Henry Dawson running from the derelict Hellfire lodge shrieking, 'My soul is truly damned!'?

That's how I imagine it all, but I can be certain of only two things: firstly, that when Dad crashes through the windscreen, hundreds of shards of glass explode onto the tarmac around him. I like to imagine each shard reflecting a different image of him, like a cascading slideshow during the eternity of the few seconds that it takes for the windscreen to shatter.

The second fact is that although his car becomes a contorted concertina of twisted metal at the entrance to the forest that now surrounds the Hellfire Club, his music system still works. Because when a passing motorist finds his body up there near the summit of Montpelier, the mountain landscape is silent except for his car speakers blaring out the songs that I will spend my childhood longing to hear – my dad's foiled attempts to gain immortality.

THREE

Joey

September 2009

You can do this, Joey, I told myself. Don't panic, don't show them that you're scared. You're not the first guy to ever walk down a busy school corridor into a new classroom full of strangers. But I was scared because not only was I changing school, I was also hoping to change my life. It was eight days after my sixteenth birthday. I had a new school uniform, a school bag filled with new books and a head filled with bad memories of last being in a classroom. In my previous school I had been bullied and ridiculed, but here in Stradbrook College I was going to keep myself to myself. This was my plan. The plan only lasted as long as it took me to meet Shane O'Driscoll.

Even if I had been the coolest guy on the planet I'd feel nervous walking into an unfamiliar classroom, crammed with faces that already knew each other and shared in-jokes and nicknames. But I wasn't cool: I was probably the uncoolest guy I knew. When God was doling out coolness I must have popped out to the bathroom or else I had been standing at the heavenly queue where you complain about being short-changed in the looks department.

I tried to conceal my nervousness as a shoal of faces turned to scrutinise the new boy in the doorway. Their glances were more dismissive than curious, but there was no hostility in anyone's eyes. I was too ordinary for them to bother interrupting their first-morning-back-at-school chatter after the summer holidays. I could already spot some cliques. In one corner, a few apprentice goths consoled each other at having to wear their school uniforms again. In another corner, sporting jocks compared bruises picked up on the rugby pitch as they swapped tales of vitamin supplements, iron-pumping and dubious sexual conquests. Two potential applicants for Young Scientist of the Year were examining what was either an old science paper or the blueprint for a homemade nuclear bomb. But the vast majority of my new classmates in Stradbrook College looked fairly laid back. The place was ethnically mixed and co-religious. It seemed to have just about everything except a single classmate who enjoyed the music I liked playing. I was an expert on the musical tastes of everyone present, because over the previous two weeks I had hacked my way into their Facebook pages. It meant that I knew who was dating whom, who was no longer dating whom and who was rumoured to secretly want to date whom. Indeed, the web was so littered with candid pictures of my new classmates clowning around at parties over the summer that I could even put names on most of the students present.

Nobody in this classroom could do the same with me, because even if they had bothered to Google me, they would not have found me online. I had taken down my Facebook page some months previously. It was not the constant cyber-bullying from the boys in my old school that had got to me, but the boringly repetitive nature of their insults. Even when it came to character assassination, nobody in the all-male school I'd attended had had enough spark to leave an original comment. I don't want to give the impression that I had been some type of odd-ball loner in my previous school: I'd been popular enough there in a dorkish way, or at least I'd encountered no great hassle until I entered that talent contest. I had learned to blend in on the edge of cliques so that it looked like I belonged. But, in truth, I never fitted in, and not because I was any sort of geek. I didn't fit in because my former classmates bored the pants off me. They were obsessed with football and manufactured bands and with throwing shapes like poor imitations of third-rate, bad-ass, not-very-fly-for-a-white-guy rappers.

Still, I had knocked along OK, even if most of those lads had considered me a bit of a sap and I had thought them a harmless bunch of cretins. That was until the bullying started after the talent contest. They might have all seen themselves as stags, but they had the herd mentality of cows. This caused me to get trampled on a lot during my final months in that school.

That was why I had promised myself that in Stradbrook I would never stand out like a fool again. There seemed to be no danger of that anyway, because few in the classroom paid me any attention as I hesitated in the doorway. Most people who glanced towards me looked away again. But one girl with jet-black hair smiled shyly in welcome from her desk beside the window. I smiled back and she grinned and looked away. I didn't recognise her features from any pictures on Facebook, but her smile was enough to boost my shaky confidence as I tried to decide what to do next. Should I try to blend in with some group, hoping they might acknowledge me? Or stake my claim to the tempting empty window seat behind the black-haired girl, where I could pretend to look busy by taking out my school-books and try not to show how flustered I was?

I was about to claim this empty desk when I sensed the atmosphere change. People were staring in my direction again. I was unused to being stared at and needed to resist an urge to glance down and check if my fly was open. Could a joker have already scrawled 'class geek' in lipstick on my forehead? But I saw no ridicule in this new scrutiny. Instead – and especially in the eyes of some girls – I felt a sense of being made to feel welcome and almost being made to feel good-looking. It was not a sensation I was used to, and I couldn't understand the sudden change in attitude. Only one girl played no part in this newly-formed adoration society: the girl with jet-black hair. She was staring at me again, unsmilingly now, almost as if she was seeing a ghost.

Then a slight movement in the doorway made me realise that it was not me that people were looking at. They were staring through me as if I was invisible.

Their eyes were drawn to a boy with a black leather jacket over his top, who had just entered the room. There seemed to be nothing particularly athletic or handsome about him, but he had an amused air of confidence and experience that was quietly mesmerising. He had the look of a guy who had already seen everything in life and had declined to buy the T-shirt. He must be the class captain, I decided; their natural leader. If I was going to be bullied here, then he would instigate it. But I sensed that I would not be bullied, because this guy would not allow anything so uncouth to occur in his class. My new classmates would take their cue from him and ignore me, because this is what he did as he brushed past.

But then, when he opened his mouth, I realised that nobody present knew who he was, except perhaps for the black-haired girl because of the way she quickly turned away. However, I could sense him already casting a spell on every other student present.

'I'm Shane O'Driscoll,' he announced quietly, 'I'm the new boy. Did I hear there's an initiation ritual that involves sacrificing a live chicken?'

Amid the laughter, one girl asked where he'd got his leather jacket.

'I stole it off a Polish sailor in Captain America's in Dún Laoghaire. The poor sap is wandering around wearing a blazer from my last school in England.' Shane turned, as if only now aware of my presence. 'You all right there, pal? Are you married to that doorframe or just going steady?'

'It's our first date.'

I felt grateful when the class laughed because he laughed.

'Well, I warn you, her jokes are bound to be wooden.'

Shane strolled towards the desk that I had wanted and then looked back.

'Sorry, what's your name?'

'Joey. Joey Kilmichael.'

'You don't normally sit over here by the window, do you, Joey?'

'No, actually,' I began, 'but ...'

'That's cool. I bags it so.' The black-haired girl kept her back turned as he occupied the desk behind her, leaving me to find an empty desk at the back of the classroom. Shane looked at the girl's stiff shoulders.

'How's it going there, Geraldine?' he asked.

She ignored his greeting. Shane shrugged as if amused and savoured the window view that should have been mine. He didn't pretend to look busy. He looked so laid-back that changing schools might be an everyday amusement. As he had a Dublin accent, I wondered why his last school had been in England. I should have felt resentful towards him for taking my desk, but instead I envied him for being the type of chilled-out person that I could never be. Shane had the relaxed charm that people said my late father had possessed. He gave the impression of being older than sixteen, of being interested in everything yet impressed by nothing. If I had one wish at that moment it was simple: I could never wish to be as cool as him so I wished for the next best thing – that somehow, Shane might pick me to become his dim-witted but faithful sidekick.

FOUR

Shane

June 2007

In that summer when he turned fourteen, Shane O'Driscoll had no desire to move to Blackrock from the cosy two-bedroom terraced house which had always been his home in Sallynoggin. But Shane would have endured any move if it stopped his parents from arguing. The move to Blackrock didn't stop their arguments though. At night he felt mortified that their new neighbours on either side of the luxury duplex townhouse at Sion Hill could overhear the rows about bills and money. During the daytime, this mortification and his own shyness made him keep his head down, reluctant to make eye contact with anyone when he crossed the landscaped gardens that divided the Sion Hill development from the constant snarl of traffic on the Rock Road. So he mostly observed his new neighbours from a distance as they reversed into designated parking spaces and emerged from BMWs and SUVs with designer-label shopping bags from the Frascati Centre. Sometimes there were teenagers in tow in Ugg boots and Abercrombie hoodies and with teeth so perfect that the kids looked like they had been enrolled for orthodontic treatment while still in the womb.

But beyond exchanging the odd checking-each-other-out glance with some of the other kids, he had no contact with anyone.

It was only three miles from Sallynoggin to Blackrock, and many working-class families — including Shane's grandparents — had originally moved there from Blackrock when the new Council estates were built in Sallynoggin half a century ago. But it seemed to Shane that there were no working-class parts of Blackrock left any more. Even the small terraces of Victorian cottages near the seafront had been tastefully modernised and upgraded. Cramped bedrooms where children once slept head to toe and four and five to a bed were now transformed into architects' studios and treatment rooms for holistic medicine. Everywhere Shane walked in those early weeks in Blackrock, he saw signs of money — discreetly coded or extravagantly brazen — and it was money that he knew his parents did not have. While he could not fault any of his new neighbours, he was cautious about letting any of them get close to him. They seemed nice as they came and went in their large cars, but he wasn't sure if their niceness was a subtle way to let him know that he was not as nice as them and that his family didn't belong in Sion Hill.

The only acquaintance he made there was an older teenager called Simon Wallace. Even these occasional conversations when their paths crossed were desultory. Wallace, who seemed an oddball, only talked to Shane in his half-sneering way because he had no one else to talk to. Wallace dressed like he could never decide whether he was into goth or emo and claimed to be the lead singer in a band too experimental to play gigs or do anything except hang out in a garage that the drummer's rich father had converted into a rehearsal studio. Shane and Simon Wallace would chat awkwardly for a few minutes whenever they met. Wallace once invited Shane to share a bottle of Southern Comfort, hinting that he knew a great drinking place nearby where nobody would disturb them. Shane made an excuse; he didn't drink and couldn't bear an entire afternoon of Wallace boasting about being suspended from school for having drugs on him and how only his parents' connections had prevented him from being expelled.

Shane didn't want to make any trouble for his own parents because they had enough troubles already. He knew that his mum and dad both loved him, but during the past year they seemed too stressed to do anything except snap at each other and snap at him. He did not recall any such simmering tensions when he was growing up in the Sallynoggin house that had originally been his grandfather's home. He could still remember his father's father, Jack O'Driscoll, living with them – a good-tempered old man who sat in an armchair all day and claimed that Shane was the spit of him as a boy. Before Shane even went to school, Grandad Jack had taught him to write by copying the old man's absolutely perfect copperplate handwriting. Jack had loved to tell Shane stories about his own childhood growing up in Blackrock; about how he started his working life in a small dairy on Castledawson Avenue, employed by a Mrs McCormack – a sour snob with the sharpest tongue and the meanest purse strings in Black-rock.

The only good thing to come from working in that dairy, Grandad Jack used to say, was that he met his wife, Molly, there. Molly had been working as a kitchen maid for Mrs McCormack. Shane's grandad had told him a million stories about the salt-of-the-earth folk and the flint-hearted snobs whom he had met in equal measure when he left McCormack's dairy to work as a messenger boy for Findlater's on Blackrock's main street. He used to cycle out to deliver groceries to the big houses in the countryside around Mount Merrion and Stillorgan. The village of his boyhood might have utterly changed, but Shane's grandad always claimed that – unlike the blow-ins who now lived there in fancy estates – the O'Driscolls had Blackrock blood in their veins for generations, flowing back to the time the village was called Newtown-by-the-Black-Rock and consisted of just a few dwellings hugging the coastline that used to be dominated by a reef of black rock out at sea.

It was five years since Shane's grandfather died. Al-though there had been occasional rows at home, Shane could remember his parents generally being happy together, putting their arms around each other and around him. Sometimes his mother had complained about the Sallynoggin house being cramped, but Shane had loved those small, cosy rooms that felt like home. Shane's dad had seemed happy in Sallynoggin too, until a year ago, when all of this changed because his dad had become gripped by an obsessive urge to move to Blackrock – a desire which had torn apart Shane's old life.

His mum could not complain about a lack of space in this Sion Hill duplex built on the site of an old convent. It was an ultra-modern development, but the high, coved ceilings were meant to evoke a gracious, bygone age. The townhouse had oak floorboards and internal doors with brass handles and coloured panes of glass that allowed light to flood into every room. There were limestone-tiled walls in the bathroom and a Victorian-style bathtub with lion's claws for legs. In the living room was an antique-style marble fireplace with a coal-effect gas fire. A purpose-built granite kitchen table with matching stools set off the built-in appliances in the kitchen. Large doors opened onto a south-facing balcony. Indeed, most of the rooms had panoramic views across Dublin Bay to Howth Head. Directly across the busy Rock Road, Shane could see Blackrock Park and the entrance to Emmet Square, the courtyard of small Edwardian terraced houses from which his grandfather once set off for work in McCormack's dairy.

The duplex felt huge. Every room had an echo because, apart from the built-in fixtures that the previous owners had left behind, the rooms remained unfurnished. A removals van had transported their old furniture from Sallynoggin, but what seemed cosy in their former home looked shabby in these spacious rooms. Shane's parents had no money to buy anything new.

There was lots of space in the duplex, but still nowhere to go to escape from his parents' arguments. No matter what room he locked himself into at night to try and block out their rows by reading a library book, their angry voices intruded through the walls and stripped away any sense of security Shane could muster. *J272.534*

Shane's days were lonely, but sleep offered little comfort because his dreams always seemed to involve water. He had one recurring nightmare where he found himself kneeling above a pool in a cellar or a cave: the sort of place where nobody would find your body if you drowned. The dream invariably ended with a sickening sensation of toppling forward, knowing that the water was so deep and ice-cold that escape was impossible. He would wake, drenched in sweat and with his heart thumping, just before his body broke the surface of the water. Shane never told his parents about these nightmares because they were preoccupied with real worries.

In his first months in Blackrock, he kept his feelings to himself. But it was the loneliness that he found hardest to endure, especially when the school holidays started and his parents left for work each morning. The only good thing about those long summer mornings and empty afternoons was that there was no simmering tension in the duplex. His parents felt guilty about leaving him alone and talked about enrolling him in summer camps, but camps cost money and Shane was relieved when the plans petered out.

Every evening when his folks came home Shane lied about the new friends that he claimed to have made playing soccer in Blackrock Park. He told them that he was enjoying the best summer of his life because this was what they needed to hear. He would have told them any lies to avoid more rows, but in reality, after three months in Blackrock he had yet to make a single friend. The local kids hanging around Blackrock Park or the Frascati Centre were not unfriendly, but they all knew each other and Shane was an outsider, nervous of ridicule and aware that his parents did not fit in.

It was madness for his parents to purchase a house that they could obviously not afford, but his father had refused to listen to logic once he became gripped by this oppressive desire to move to Blackrock. In the end, Shane's mother was browbeaten by his father's talk and – as she frequently complained – by the fact that he had lied to her and to everyone else about the figures involved. It was only when signing the deeds in the solicitor's office that she became aware of how enormous their mortgage was: the monthly repayments would eat up every cent they earned.

Shane's father was an eternal optimist, always convinced that his latest get-rich-quick scheme would make their fortune. He could sell snow to Eskimos. The problem was that the Eskimos would send the snow back or their cheque would bounce or he would suddenly decide that there was no future in selling snow but he could make a fortune by selling sand to Arabs in the desert instead.

Now, whenever Shane's father outlined his latest money-making scheme, Shane's mum would wearily raise her eyes to heaven and he would look across at Shane for support. Shane always said, 'That sounds brilliant, Dad,' because he sensed that his dad desperately needed somebody to still believe in him, and Shane desperately wanted to believe.

Only once, when saying goodnight to Shane one night, had his dad let this mask of optimism drop. The man looked so exhausted that Shane asked, 'Dad, why did we really move to Blackrock?'

His father lay on the bed beside him, staring at the ceiling for a long time before replying, 'This is where your grandad was born. And both his father and grandfather were born in the small mud-wall cabins that used to line Castledawson Avenue. They were knocked down when the priests extended the grounds of Blackrock College. Every night during the last year we lived in Sallynoggin, your grandad's voice kept coming between me and my sleep, whispering in my head that I should bring you back to Blackrock.'

'But why here in Sion Hill, Dad? I mean, we can't afford this house.'

'Because some things are more important than money. I'll find the money somehow. I looked at cheaper houses, but none were this high up.'

'What's the point in being this high up? We're just paying extra for the sea view.'

'The view has nothing to do with it, Shane. The minute

I walked in here, I knew it was the house your grandad wanted me to buy, no matter what it cost, because you would be safe here.'

'Safe from what?'

Shane's dad looked embarrassed, his eyes jaded from lack of sleep. 'Safe from drowning, son. I know it makes no sense, but I was convinced that if we stayed in Sallynoggin, our house would be flooded.'

'Dad, our old house wasn't even near a river.'

His father shrugged. 'Maybe it's all madness, but I couldn't shake the notion from my head. Every night, after I'd finally fall asleep, I'd dream that there was a hidden pool of water under the foundations of our old house; that while we slept, it would start to seep through the floorboards and lap up the stairs. I used to wake up terrified that your bedroom was flooded, and by the time I reached you, you'd be floating there in your pyjamas, already drowned and lost to us.'

FIVE

Joey's Mother

1993

Music is pounding from the speakers in the living room when my mum wakes from a drunken slumber. Every night has been the same in the three months since my father died. Every night she has sat up until dawn with a vodka bottle and a rough cut of his unfinished album to keep her company. Hearing his voice now as she wakes sends a shiver down her spine. The demo tapes bring her no comfort but only make the ache of his absence worse and cause her to drink even more to try and dull that ache. The sitting-room table has a bundle of posters of my father on it. He is holding a guitar, his face lit by a spotlight. The words 'Appearing at …' are printed on each poster, followed by a blank space. She has lost track of all the tiny venues whose names she had had to write into that blank space as he criss-crossed Ireland, stubbornly trying to build an audience for a style that was uniquely his own. He never played big venues, except as a support act with half the audience ignoring him. But she remembers the excitement of small gigs where he electrified audiences with a sound they had never heard before.

It is a sound that she decides she never wants to hear again, because if she keeps playing that tape over and over she will keep on drinking vodka alone in the dark, slurring her words, blacking in and out of consciousness, hating herself for becoming a drunken lush, an alcoholic. Rising unsteadily, she walks into the bedroom they once shared to stare down at me sleeping in my cot. She knows that I will wake soon and will need to be fed; she knows that yesterday her hands shook so much that she almost dropped me. This spiral into chaos cannot continue, the nights without sleep, the days without seeing a soul, the filth and squalor in this cottage where she can no longer bring herself to cook or bathe her child or do anything except cry. She knows that she must choose between being Dessie Kilmichael's widow and being a mother to his child.

How long does she spend standing over my cot, shaking with grief, shaking with desire for the oblivion of another shot of vodka? Finally, she turns and searches for the suitcase that he always brought with him on the road. Ruthlessly, she crams every reminder of him into it. Leaving me alone in my cot, she leaves Brusna Cottages and crosses Main Street. She swings left down Bath Place until she reaches Idrone Terrace with the train tracks and the sea before her. It is raining heavily when she climbs the old footbridge over the railway tracks and stands there for a long time gazing down. There, she hurls all of my father's demo tapes, his posters and press cuttings, his lyric sheets and every photograph of them together down onto the train tracks, watching as each precious memento is slowly scattered by the wind and the rain seeps into every handwritten lyric. She knows that this is her only way to break free of the past before the past breaks her. She stands there alone until the first train comes an hour later, until its wheels plough over the remaining traces of my father. By then, his life's work and dreams have been blown all the way down the train tracks. Finally, she walks home to pour the remaining vodka down the sink and to focus purely on the future, for my sake.

SIX

Joey

September 2009

During my first week in Stradbrook College I realised that it was not a hanging offence to be different there. But no matter how progressive the atmosphere seemed, I was determined not to let my guard down. I planned to blend into the back-ground without anyone noticing me. However, Shane O'Driscoll noticed me. During boring classes he would wink across the room. At break-time he'd slap my back and start up a conversation. Shane chatted to everyone, but when he talked to me he made it feel like we belonged to a secret club of two, sharing a private joke that no one else could grasp.

Although some people said he came from Blackrock and others that he came from Sallynoggin, he had spent the previous two years in England. The fact that he sought out my friendship confused me, because the whole class – with one exception – kept falling over themselves to be his friend. Only Geraldine, the girl who had smiled at me on that first morning, seemed immune to his spell. Geraldine was different from the other girls in the class: more mature, and yet somehow more vulnerable. She was the classmate

I talked to most. Sadly, all these conversations happened in my head, because although I longed to ask her out, I never seemed to find the right words to start such a conversation. The fact that she was the only person in class without a Facebook page made it difficult too: while I knew too much about everyone else, I knew too little about her.

Within a fortnight, Shane and I were best buddies at break-time. Yet when I tried to describe him to my mum, I realised that I knew virtually nothing about him either. He told me that both his parents had died two years ago, but when you discover that somebody is an orphan, you are terrified of asking the wrong question in case you touch a raw nerve. Whenever I did ask Shane about his life, he side-stepped my questions by turning his replies into jokes, and soon I would be telling him even more about myself, because he was a good listener. He seemed fascinated, almost greedy for every detail of my life.

'What was the hassle in your old school?' he asked me at break one morning.

'It was all about soul,' I said, leaning against the wall. 'My ex-classmates had no soul and I had too much of it.'

'You only have one soul,' Shane said, 'unless you steal someone else's.'

'When I say soul,' I explained, 'I mean soul music. My father used to sing it.'

'And he doesn't any more?'

'He died in a car crash in the Dublin mountains. He was coming home from a gig. He was a singer-songwriter.'

'Was he any good?'

I shrugged. 'If you Google him you find weird mentions of him. Some guy blogging, "It was hearing the maverick genius Dessie Kilmichael that inspired me to start playing guitar." Or, "This dude sounds like a new Dessie Kilmichael – what a tragedy his death was, when songwriters with a fraction of his talent are now millionaires."'

'And what do you think of his songs?' Shane asked.

'I've never heard them.'

He laughed in disbelief and kicked a pebble across the yard. 'You're kidding me.'

'No. He even had a name for his debut album – *New Town Soul* – but he never got around to releasing it. He was constantly tinkering with it, doing different takes on every track. Mum says he was looking for the perfect take, the one that would make him immortal. She destroyed his demo tapes when I was small.'

'Why?' Shane looked up.

I shrugged, unwilling to go into too much detail. At times I knew that Mum still yearned for the companionship of vodka. Occasionally, as a child, I had found an unopened bottle under her bed and knew that she was struggling against the temptation to open it. She always overcame that temptation, though I would see the strain in her for days afterwards. 'She just did,' I replied. 'She rarely talks about him.'

'Do you miss him?'

'I never knew him. I was only a baby when he died. I

went through his old record collection, though. Mum kept those, though she never played them. They sort of became my way of getting to know him, if you see what I mean. Some of the records are so old, I think he must have owned them at my age, when he was just learning to play guitar.'

'So, do you play yourself?'

'Don't get me started.' I raised my eyes sheepishly to heaven. 'Why do you think I got such grief in my old school?'

'What do you mean? How could playing a guitar cause hassle?'

'It depends on what you play,' I said. 'I taught myself to play. I used to sit in my bedroom and imagine my dad picking out tabs at my age. It's crazy, but I'd spend hours writing songs and playing them with my eyes closed, imagining that somehow Dad was listening, that he was my imaginary audience of one.'

'You could do far worse.' Shane spoke so quietly that I knew he was thinking about his own dead father.

'I did do far worse,' I replied. 'I entered a talent contest in my old school.'

'What's so wrong with that?'

'It was more like a karaoke contest – lads dancing to rap tracks and their girlfriends copying routines from girl bands. It wasn't about talent; it was about conformity, being a pale imitation of some celebrity. In a school where you get bullied for wearing the wrong sort of trainers, what sort of moron walks out on stage with just a guitar and a page of dodgy handwritten lyrics?'

'I bet your lyrics were good,' Shane said.

'Survival in that school wasn't about being good, it was about not standing out. You needed to always wear the same clothes as everyone else, never express an original thought or leave yourself open to ridicule. I remember the awful silence when I walked on stage in that hall packed with boys and their girlfriends – or their sisters dragged along to look like girlfriends. My voice dried up and my guitar went out of tune. I knew that all I could expect from then on was to be bullied and made a joke of.'

'Not all schools are like that,' Shane said. 'This place isn't.'

'I never intend to find out,' I replied, as the bell went for the end of break. 'I'm not sticking my head up to let any hard men give me a kicking because they feel I need to be put back in my place. The guys in my old school knew I had no dad to turn to and that I'd say nothing to my mum because she had enough worries of her own.'

'How bad was it?' Shane asked quietly, as we joined the stream of pupils heading indoors.

'Just taunts and jeers at first,' I said. 'Pages ripped from copybooks, insults scrawled on walls, my lunch stolen or my mobile phone stuffed down a toilet bowl. But soon even the geeks were joining in, because if somebody else was being bullied they wouldn't be targeted themselves. In the end I couldn't hide the strain – or the bruises – when I got beaten up. Mum was great, eating the head off the principal when he just waffled on about the school's anti-bullying policy. He promised suspensions but she told him to stop talking rubbish because the ringleaders' fathers were too well-connected for the school to have the guts to expel them. She told him to stuff his school. Then, somehow, she pulled strings to get me in here.'

We reached the door into the corridor. Shane stopped and looked at me. 'Your mum sounds like a good woman. You're lucky.'

'She's more than just my mum,' I said, as we went inside. 'She's my best friend.' I paused. 'Listen, Shane, don't mention this stuff to anyone. Here in Stradbrook I just want to keep my head down, OK?'

SEVEN

Shane

June 2007

That summer he turned fourteen, Shane would smile sleepily and lie to his folks about his plans for the day ahead when they woke him before leaving for work every morning. But the only event he could truly look forward to was his morning visit to Blackrock Library. His day depended on the success of this visit, because he could cope with the long afternoons spent alone if he had a good adventure story to lose himself in. There was only so much television a fourteen-year-old could watch, the new Xbox his father promised him after his old one broke had never materialised and Shane rarely got any texts on his mobile, because his old pals in Sallynoggin were too busy getting on with their own lives to bother checking out his new one. Once or twice, he took a bus back to Sallynoggin and tried to hang out on the green opposite his old house, but he got too much grief from some older lads. They jeered that he had become a snob because he'd gone to live in Blackrock.

Now, his routine was simple. After each library visit he would go for a long solitary walk around Blackrock or out the Booterstown Road to where a tiny, overgrown cemetery was hidden behind an Esso garage. It was a good place to sit alone without any passers-by thinking he was a loser. Sometimes he would walk up the narrow cul-de-sac at Castledawson Avenue to stand outside the deserted ruin of Mrs McCormack's dairy where his grand-parents first met when they were his age. The front door looked like it hadn't been opened for years and the frayed lace curtains behind the unlit windows were blackened with grime. At times he felt a longing to explore the empty rooms of that house, but a fear held him back, the fore-boding sense of terror which he felt if he even put his hand on the dilapidated wooden gate.

He would turn for home feeling utterly alone, but the frightening thing was that some afternoons when he returned to the duplex, he did not feel truly alone there. A newly-built development like Sion Hill could not have ghosts, but sometimes he had the sensation that unseen eyes were watching him move from room to room. The duplex seemed unnaturally cold on such afternoons and, even if it was raining, he would sit out on the balcony be-cause he felt safer there. He would try to immerse himself in a library book until he heard his mother's key in the lock.

No book could be a substitute for what he yearned for, which was to make a friend. But it was through books that he met Geraldine. As that summer wore on, they were often the only two people scouring the shelves of Black-rock Library in the sweltering heat. She was the same age as Shane, but she looked dead cool for a girl. She was tomboyish, but very definitely female in all the right places.

She looked like someone he could talk to, but he was too shy to start a conversation. Geraldine always arrived and left alone. Shane sensed that she had no shortage of friends but loved to spend a part of each day lost in a book.

Geraldine had jet-black hair and a slightly bossy air. She would browse contentedly until she found a book she liked and then stand between the library stacks, smiling as if entranced by the opening paragraph, before closing the book with a satisfied snap and disappearing back out into the sunlight, unaware that Shane was there, unable to stop staring at her. He started to automatically borrow whatever books she left back, even if he had read them a dozen times before. This was his way of getting to know her, to feel that – unbeknownst to her – he was sharing in some tiny part of her life. Soon, he even began to follow her home – discreetly, from a safe distance – because in his mind it prolonged the time when they were together and it put off the loneliness of heading back to the empty duplex that he still couldn't think of as home.

Geraldine lived in the last house on a small old redbrick terrace just off the end of Newtown Avenue. There was nothing grand about the house, just like there was nothing grand about Geraldine. But the house looked inviting, like the sort of home he would have chosen if he had been given any say in this move to Blackrock. It had a side garden with a wrought iron gate and, once, after Geraldine went indoors, Shane peered through the bars and saw a hammock suspended between an apple tree and the wall. That night, when his parents argued so loudly that he couldn't even read, he closed his eyes and tried to imagine himself swaying peacefully in that hammock.

On the fifth morning that he followed her home, Geraldine stopped outside her gate and stared back down the road while Shane ducked behind a parked car. When he glanced up cautiously, she was still standing there, waiting for him to emerge. Feeling mortified, he stood up and walked away without looking back. That night, no matter how hard he tried to focus on his book, nothing could block out the sounds of his parents arguing. He felt that he had lost the only friend he had – even if Geraldine had never known that he viewed her as his friend and that he would spend lonely afternoons imagining scenarios where they became buddies, taking turns to sway in that hammock in her garden.

The next morning, he felt ashamed when Geraldine came into the library. He was afraid she would call him a creep. But she just returned a new mystery book and left without glancing in his direction. When Shane snatched up the book, he noticed a slip of paper sticking out. The handwriting was neat in the way that only a girl's hand-writing could be:

> *I bet you think you're the shiest person on the planet but I would win that prize because I'm shier. Why don't you text me what you think of this book? I think the ending is savage.*
> *Geraldine.*

Underneath this message she had drawn a smiley face and jotted down her mobile number.

Shane didn't bother going back to the empty house. Sitting alone in Blackrock Park, he finished the book within two hours. He loved every word of it, partly because it was so good, but also because he knew that she had liked it. His first text was short: *It was utterly brill. Who is your fav writer?*

Texting took away the awkwardness of talking. By bedtime, they had exchanged two dozen messages. He barely even heard his parents argue that night. When he found it hard to sleep, it was not because of any fears of recurring nightmares about water; it was because Geraldine had agreed to meet him outside Blackrock Library the next morning and Shane felt that maybe he had found the friend he was longing for.

EIGHT

Joey

October 2009

Six weeks into our autumn term, my new class at Stradbrook College attended an overnight retreat in a centre in Glencree in the mountains. On the way, we stopped off at the burned-out ruins of the Hell-fire Club. The others all shrieked and tried to spook each other as they chased through the remote, tumbledown rooms. Only Shane stayed outside the old hunting lodge, sitting on a stump in the forest. When people called on him to join them he would grin and shake his head, but there was something about his eyes that was the closest I had ever come to seeing him scared.

I sat beside him, partly to keep him company but also because I was upset. This was the road where my father had died. Shane looked up after a while.

'Can you imagine the sickening taste of raw whiskey and melted butter?' he asked. 'That's what the Hellfire Club members used to drink, toasting the devil in front of a blazing fire when they came up here, roaring drunk, from the Eagle Tavern.'

'And to think that us teenagers get a bad name if we

drink a few cans in the park on a Friday night,' I joked, trying to lighten his mood.

'A Blackrock man once died up here,' Shane said. 'Henry Dawson. His servant boy claimed that he'd found him with his throat cut. The same servant boy wound up owning half of Blackrock.'

'Who the hell was Henry Dawson?'

'A gambler with nothing left to gamble, the sort of man that people say couldn't resist one last bet with the devil.' Shane picked up a loose stone and hurled it into the undergrowth. 'He was the last of the family who built Castledawson House. He came into his inheritance too young and blazed through it too soon. In the end he was a wreck from lust and drink and opium, with nothing left except a body wracked by illness and a house riddled with debt.'

I had never heard Shane speak this way before. 'When did this happen?' I asked.

Shane glanced towards the ruins. 'Several lifetimes ago.'

'So, how do you know all this?'

'An old doctor once told me. He warned me to never let anyone steal my soul.'

That sounded crazy to me. 'How could anyone steal your soul?'

'That's what I asked Dr Thomson.' Shane rose. 'Let's get back on the bus; this place gives me the creeps – too many bad memories. I can't stand being near any house that was burned down.'

Finally the rest of the class was herded up and only when we left the wood did Shane's normal good humour return. Soon he had the rest of us in stitches, teasing girls-impersonating teachers, razor-sharp and yet laid back as he won the most outlandish bets with people about every-thing from the number of sheep in the next field to the colour of the next car we would pass.

When we reached the retreat centre we had group exercises for the rest of the day. We had to act out impro-vised dramas about immigration and, later, we were paired off, taking turns at being blindfolded so we could learn to trust the person leading us. Some of the exercises seemed ridiculous, but my new class were willing to go with the flow, never losing their sense of humour. They didn't turn it all into a farce either, though. I don't know what my former classmates would have done. Either die of embar-rassment or wreck the building probably.

After dinner we were left to ourselves. Shane had insisted that I bring along my guitar. Two other lads had brought guitars, and soon we were enjoying a singsong. I was unused to playing in front of people, but it felt OK because all the songs were chart hits that everyone knew. It was midnight when Shane raised his hand for silence.

'Mademoiselles and morons, damsels and damsellettes, in our midst we have a great singer-songwriter and poet. Remember where you heard his songs first because one day you will spend hard-earned cash for the privilege of hearing this dude play. Now give it up for Joey Kilmichael.'

I stared at Shane, feeling shocked and betrayed. He

knew that I didn't want to sing or let anyone know that I wrote songs. After my previous experience, the last thing I needed was more ridicule. But the faces around me were not mocking. Every student seemed to pick up and unconsciously mirror the interest in Shane's eyes. They wanted to hear my lyrics. Shane gave me a wink that seemed to say, Go for it, kid. Stand up and be counted.

His wink gave me strength. Closing my eyes, I played the opening chords. But it wasn't my father that I imagined as my audience this time – it was Shane. I could sense him enjoying the music and could feel his enthusiasm spreading like an infection among my classmates. My lyrics were about vulnerability, about what it felt like to be young, to be excited by and yet slightly scared of all the new emotions I kept encountering.

The silence when I sang was different from that awful silence during the talent contest. It felt like I had stopped time and I had people in my spell. My voice soared. For the first time I felt I truly understood the buzz of performing that had lured my father to trek across Ireland and Europe. Normally I was shy and tongue-tied, but behind this guitar I became another person to whom the old rules no longer applied. When I finished the first song, my classmates applauded and demanded more. I sang four more of my songs and then finally I put down my guitar, embarrassed by such acclaim. Shane winked again and I knew that he had orchestrated this because he knew I needed to be brought out of my shell. I had felt safe singing because Shane would never allow jeering. With a shock I realised that, just now, Shane felt like a father figure.

Then the singsong resumed, with the whole class joining in on songs that everyone knew. I left the other two guitarists at it. People gave me appreciative thumbs-up signs as I walked towards the open doorway. I heard footsteps and thought that Shane was following. But when I glanced back the person following me out into the night air was Geraldine. Silently we stared out across the valley. The stars were so bright up here, the air still. I could sense her body like I always sensed it when she was near me. She was the most beautiful girl I had ever seen, her skin with its own special scent. I didn't know what to say but it was she who spoke.

'I liked your songs.'

'Thanks.'

'The lyrics were brilliant. How do you make them up?'

'They just come into my head; it's a bit of a mystery.'

She shivered slightly. 'I don't like mysteries.'

'How do you mean?'

'I like things to make sense, to be uncomplicated. Like you.'

'Are you calling me stupid?'

'Uncomplicated doesn't mean stupid,' Geraldine said. 'An uncomplicated person is someone you can trust, not someone you think you know who turns out to be a totally different type of person.'

'Are you talking about Shane?'

'I'm just telling you to watch yourself, because you're better than Shane.'

I shrugged, embarrassed. 'What's so special about me?'

'I'm not saying there's anything special about you.'

'But you must admit there's something special about Shane.'

'Something unnatural, more like.'

'What do you mean?'

'I knew him two summers ago. He was a bit like you, back then.'

'In what way?'

Geraldine blushed. 'He was kinda cute … just ordinary, but he was sweet.' She stopped and looked at me. 'He's using you.'

'What do you mean? Before I hung out with Shane nobody in this class knew I existed.'

'I noticed you the moment you walked in.'

'Why?'

She turned away, embarrassed. 'Are you fishing for compliments or something?'

'I'm just not used to girls chatting me up.'

'I'm not chatting you up.' Geraldine sounded defensive. 'Being able to sing a couple of songs doesn't make you a rock star. I've never chased any boy in my life.'

'I didn't mean it like that,' I said quickly. 'Listen, Geraldine, I'm no good at saying things except in songs. But I think about you all the time. I keep trying to find the courage to ask you out.'

'Don't waste your breath, because I'll say no.' She saw how crushed I looked and brushed my arm softly. 'That sounds cold, but I'm not ready to go out with another boy just yet. Bitter experience; let's not go into it.'

'Has it to do with Shane?'

'I thought I knew him.' She paused, seeking the right words. 'Then one day he changed. Does he ever mention his folks?'

'Just that they died and he went to live with an aunt in England. When she got sick he came back to Dublin.'

'Do you remember a fire two years ago in the duplex development at Sion Hill?'

It took me a minute to recall watching coverage of the aftermath on the news, but I couldn't remember any details of it.

'Is that how they died?'

'That was the dream home his folks couldn't afford,' Geraldine said. 'His mum died of smoke inhalation. His dad dragged her dead body outside, then he kept screaming that Shane was still in there, though the whole place was in flames by then. The neighbours couldn't hold him back. He charged straight back in, shouting that he had to save his son from drowning – it sounded mad in the middle of a fire. The roof collapsed on him moments later.' Geraldine glanced at me. 'Do you know where Shane was all that time?'

I shook my head.

'Standing unnoticed amid the crowd in his pyjamas, saying nothing as he watched his dad run back inside to his death.'

NINE

Shane

June 2007

When Shane and Geraldine met in Blackrock on the morning after they had first sent texts to each other it was like they needed to make up for all the times when they had said nothing. Now, they couldn't stop talking and laughing. The librarian didn't know what had got into them, but they didn't stay in the library for any longer than it took to pick some books. Soon they were walking along Newtown Avenue. This time when Geraldine went in through the side gate to her garden Shane walked alongside her. Everything felt new and thrilling and when he touched the hammock beside the apple tree Geraldine laughed at the sense of wonder on his face.

'It's only an ordinary hammock, silly,' she said. 'Surely you've seen a hammock before?'

But for Shane there was nothing ordinary about her garden. It felt almost as if a guardian angel had led him here, as if someone who understood his loneliness had granted him his second most fervent wish. His most fervent wish remained that his parents would find enough money to be happy. But this morning, he wanted to forget about any problems at home and to savour the sense of being made to feel welcome in Geraldine's garden as her grandmother appeared at the back door.

'Stay out there in the sunshine,' the woman said with a smile. 'You both look like you wouldn't say no to some crisps and lemonade.'

Shane spent all afternoon lying in Geraldine's garden, while she burned him a CD of her favourite songs and let him share her earphones so that they could both listen to her iPod. She kept disappearing into the house to get books he hadn't read. She even brought out a cartoon strip that she had drawn herself, with matchstick figures spouting such utter nonsense that the captions sent Shane and Geraldine into unstoppable fits of laughter. It was late afternoon when Geraldine produced a battered biscuit tin that contained her treasure trove of most precious possessions.

Shane sensed that she had never shown some of these mementos to another living soul. There were ticket stubs from concerts by her favourite bands, a worn leather collar belonging to her dog that had died in her arms and a cherished wristwatch that once belonged to her mother, who drowned in a swimming accident off the Blackrock coast when Geraldine was only three years old.

'Nobody could ever explain it,' Geraldine said. 'My mother had been a Leinster schoolgirls champion swimmer. She even won an athletics scholarship to an American university. People talked of her being an Irish Olympic swimming prospect. I sort of got in the way.'

'How do you mean?' Shane asked.

Geraldine fidgeted awkwardly with the strap of the watch. 'She came home from a summer job in London two months pregnant. A summer romance that didn't last. I was her only souvenir of it. After I was born, she had to give up the swimming scholarship. She wound up back here in Blackrock, living with her mum. She still went swimming every day, though. She was training for a sea race when she died.'

'How did it happen?' Shane asked.

Geraldine put the watch back in the box. 'A freak accident, Gran says. It was a totally calm day by all accounts, and she knew this stretch of coastline like her own skin. Afterwards, if Gran brought me near water I would scream. I was terrified of water. I still am. I have dreams about drowning.'

'So do I.'

Geraldine looked at him. 'What type of dreams?'

Shane shrugged. It was impossible to explain his recurring nightmares and how his father also dreamed about water seeping up through the floorboards of their old house. 'Let's talk about something else,' he said. 'Let's talk about books. Do you ever imagine what it would be like if you were a character inside one, going around investigating mysteries and suchlike?'

Geraldine laughed, keen to move the conversation away from dark memories. 'We could do that,' she said.

'What do you mean?'

'We could start an investigating agency and solve a few mysteries.'

'Are you serious?'

'Don't be ridiculous. I just mean it as a bit of a laugh, something to do.'

Geraldine made it sound like the greatest joke in the world, but Shane knew why she suggested it. The idea appealed to her for the same reason that it appealed to him – if they ironically pretended to be detectives it would give them an excuse to hang out together, without any 'boyfriend' or 'girlfriend' pressure.

'We better invent a password,' he said with mock seriousness.

'Fair enough,' Geraldine said. 'We'll use the maker's name on my mother's watch, but only if you promise never to reveal it aloud to another living soul.'

She went indoors and fetched an envelope that she placed the watch inside. 'We'll seal it with our lips,' she said, 'and then it will be just our secret.'

Shane hoped that she was going to kiss him, but instead she wet the glue on the back of the envelope with her lips, then handed him the envelope to do the same. He followed suit and passed her back the sealed envelope.

'It's truly our secret now,' she said and blushed slightly.

He nodded and rose to leave. As he walked home, he kept remembering Geraldine's smile as she carefully stowed away that envelope in her biscuit tin of precious possessions.

TEN

Joey

Late October 2009

As the weeks went on, some teachers in Stradbrook began to harbour a mistrust of Shane. But I noticed that Geraldine didn't just mistrust him: she seemed genuinely spooked in his presence. Not that I ever got to properly ask her why, because when Shane was around she never spoke to me and, more and more, Shane seemed to be perpetually at my side.

Before the school retreat in Wicklow, people had seen me as merely his sidekick, but now I acquired the nickname of The Songwriter. Older students would stop me in the corridor to ask my opinion about different bands. Two sixth years asked me to join a band, but I had no interest in the mainstream covers they planned to do because nobody ever became immortal by sounding like somebody else. I wanted to play my own songs, because whether they were good or woeful, my songs were at least original.

Shane got a great kick out of other people liking my songs. He joked about becoming my future tour manager, whose duties would include visiting all venues in advance to check out the sound system, the drugs and the girls. I discovered that he had put up a Facebook page for him-self, but it contained no personal details, just a full-length, unsmiling picture of himself against a seascape of the Blackrock shoreline at dusk. The photo had been digitally manipulated so that directly behind his shoulder there was a line of reproductions of his face, decreasing in size and becoming ever more blurred as they stretched away into seeming infinity across the skyline. He laughed when I asked him about this picture and jokingly called it 'post-modern irony'. I had no idea what 'post-modern irony' was, but I knew this was the only answer I would get from Shane.

Shane insisted that I create a Facebook page containing all the lyrics of my songs and pictures that he took of me clowning around. He wanted to make some recordings of me to post as well. But I refused because – and maybe this was a reluctance picked up from my father – I didn't want to record any of my songs until I had got the sound as near to perfection as it could be. Shane joked that the page would improve my love life, that half the girls in our class would date any boy who could strum a guitar and all of them would date any boy who could actually play the blasted thing in tune. I was only interested in one girl though. But the next occasion we got to speak was when Geraldine and I found ourselves shoulder to shoulder as we entered the science lab, a fortnight after that Wicklow class retreat.

'Shane is using you in some way. You've become like his pet poodle.'

'Shane is sound,' I protested. 'I really don't understand

your hang-up about him. How is he using me?'

'He wants something from you and he'll get it – you wait and see. Did he tell you that he came home because his aunt in England is seriously ill?'

'Yeah.'

'She's not seriously ill; she's seriously dead.'

Geraldine selected a desk as far as possible away from me, knowing that people would automatically leave the seat beside me free for Shane. I didn't know what to make of her news or what quarrel had occurred between them to make her so mistrustful of him. When I quizzed Shane during lunch break he sounded hurt by her attitude.

'I don't know why she hates me. We were thick as thieves two summers ago, but then my folks died and my life turned upside-down. Losing your parents screws you up. After the fire I was packed off to live with my mum's sister in Leeds. I last saw Geraldine outside the church in Blackrock when the mourning car pulled away. She waved, but I didn't wave back, because nothing felt real. You know, some nights I still wake with the stink of smoke in my nostrils. When I went to England, I was convinced that my clothes stank of smoke, even though my aunt had thrown away all the clothes I brought over from Ireland. That fire killed something inside me. The last face I expected to see when I walked into this class was Geraldine's, but she cut me dead. She fancies the pants off you, though.'

'She does not,' I said, embarrassed.

'I know the signs because she fancied me once. For

you, she is seriously hot to trot. I have no chance with her because she thinks that I should still be the sad-eyed boy she last saw at that funeral. But you have to move on in life; you must overcome grief. It's time you overcame your loss.'

'What are you talking about?'

'I'm talking about how you're still mourning your dad.'

'I never even knew my dad.'

'That doesn't stop you thinking about him. Listen, I know about loneliness because I'm fatherless too. Life has kicked us both in the teeth. Now you can either curl up and die or stand up – no matter how hard you hurt inside – and show the world you're a contender.'

Shane adopted a boxer's stance, playfully punching my shoulder. 'Come on; give me your hardest punch and I'll just keep getting back up.'

His blows hurt. I slugged him back, playfully at first but then with a growing annoyance. He laughed, dodging my fists to land a hard slap on my cheek. 'You're letting your guard down, Joey, losing your cool. Never let anyone see your emotions. It gives them a glimpse into your soul.'

He caught my fist as I swung it at him again. I felt angry without being sure why. Maybe it was the way he kept mentioning my father, as if to emphasise his absence. Sensing my anger, Shane brought his face close to mine and contorted his features so that the lip hung down as if deformed. The sounds from his throat were not words, but a strangulated babble of grunts as if he couldn't speak.

His eyes looked manic. It was scary and yet so darkly funny that soon he could hold the mask no longer and we were doubled over with laughter.

'Pull that face in history class,' I said, 'and you'll give Bongo Drums Quinn a heart attack.'

The bell announced the end of break. I wanted to maintain the good vibe between us, but what Geraldine had said would not go away.

'Why did you come home from Leeds?' I asked.

'Have you seen Leeds United football team? Would you fancy having to trudge through life following that shower?'

'You told me your aunt got sick.'

'That's what I said, yes.'

'I hear that's a lie; someone said your aunt is actually dead.'

Shane's tone was casual but his eyes had grown cautious. 'What's the big deal if she is dead?'

'Why would you lie about it?'

'Is this Geraldine causing mischief? Geraldine always fancied herself as a bit of an amateur detective.'

'Is it true?'

Shane waited until a throng of students heading back into class went past us. 'My aunt died in a crash three months ago: a head-on collision with a truck. She was driving on the wrong side of a motorway.'

'Then why tell people she's ill?'

'Exactly how tragic a figure do you want me to cut, Joey? I had enough sympathy when my folks died, with everyone tiptoeing around me on eggshells. I don't need more people feeling sorry for me. I could have stayed in Leeds, but I came home because I had a few ghosts to face here.' Shane stared out the school gates. He looked older suddenly, and in that moment I sensed an intense loneliness within him. It was the first time I had heard him talk openly about his life. 'I still miss my folks. I even miss lying awake listening to them squabbling. It was money that pulled them apart, rows every time a bill came in. Mum was so sick of the stress that she used to say that the only way they would ever get out of debt was if one of them died and the other one collected the insurance pay-out.'

The yard was almost empty now. 'That was harsh,' I said as we started walking indoors.

'Unfortunately it was true. They both had large insurance policies. A small fortune came to me when they died. The house in Sion Hill was gutted, but I inherited another big insurance payout from that too. Then my aunt who died also left me everything. My solicitor jokes that I have a Midas touch when it comes to inheritance. Two summers ago my greatest wish was to be rich. I'm now rich beyond my dreams, though the money is being administered in trust for me until I'm twenty-one. But I would swap every last half-crown for company, to belong to a family.'

The phrase 'every last half-crown' struck me as odd. It belonged to another century. 'Where do you live?' I asked. 'You always avoid the question.'

'I live in a granny flat in a converted garage on Pine

Lawn. I get my meals and my washing done. All the bills get paid by my solicitor, who gives me a weekly allowance.'

'That sounds lonely.'

'It has its advantages: I'm as free as a bird.'

'Come home with me some evening,' I said. 'Mum's a good cook, she'd be glad to meet you. I don't have many pals.'

'I don't want to come between you and your mum,' Shane replied. 'After all, she is your best friend. Besides, I'm not the one you should ask home. You and Geraldine were made for each other.' We had reached our classroom. The door was shut, the history lesson already started. 'I've seen how she looks at you, Joey. Geraldine's a simmering fuse. All you have to do is find the courage to strike the match and she'll need to be scraped off you.'

Shane opened the door and the classroom went quiet as we entered. Geraldine stared up, like she knew we had been discussing her. Our history teacher, Bongo Drums Quinn, turned from writing notes on the blackboard. He had earned his nickname by endlessly boasting about his exploits as a drummer in various bands. You could spot the traits of an old rocker in him, but now he put twenty years of practised sarcasm in his voice. 'Gentlemen, you must have been discussing something important to keep you away from learning about Hitler's tyranny?'

'We were discussing our future pursuit of happiness, sir,' Shane replied.

'Really?' Bongo Drums fingered the stick of chalk as if half-tempted to fling it at Shane. 'And when will this spontaneous combustion of happiness occur?'

'The day after I collect my inheritance on my twenty-first birthday.' Shane winked at me. 'That's when Joey Kilmichael's world tour will start. We might even need a drummer, if you play your cards right. We plan to visit the sort of cities whose names used to be printed on the dials of old radio sets: cities that Joey has barely even heard of.'

ELEVEN

Shane

July and August 2007

For the rest of that summer, Geraldine and Shane met every morning at Blackrock Library. If they were feeling rich – Shane's dad insisted on leaving him pocket money, though Shane knew that the man sometimes went without lunch in work – they sat in the juice bar down Bath Avenue or in Cafe Java beside O'Rourke's pub.

Geraldine became Shane's passport into the soul of Blackrock. She seemed to know everyone, and everyone knew her. At the weekends, she introduced him to the stallholders in the Blackrock Market, the sellers of bean-bags and vintage clothes, the tarot card reader and the owners of the old curiosity shop. The two teenagers regularly came across curios when they browsed for hours in that ramshackle courtyard until the stallholders finally shooed them away, but they never encountered any mysteries there.

There were no mysteries to solve in Blackrock Park either, except the mystery of getting to know each other. They spent whole afternoons chasing one another across the playground or rolling down the grassy slopes, shrieking as they tried to tickle each other, with their limbs tangled up in mock fights. Afterwards they lay breathless side by side, staring up at the sky and inventing outlandish creatures from the shapes of passing clouds: camels riding unicycles or six-legged sheep with giraffes' necks playing xylophones. Each new invention set them off into renewed fits of giggles until Geraldine would stuff grass down Shane's neck and jump up to let him chase after her.

The only part of the park that Geraldine disliked was the ornate pond, but one afternoon in late August, she let Shane take her by the hand and lead her across the stone causeway out onto a small concrete island. The pond wasn't deep, but Shane knew that she was still scared to be surrounded on all sides by water.

'Water will be the death of me,' she said.

'Don't be silly.'

'I'm not being silly. Water killed my mother and it will kill me too. Don't ask me how I know, but I just do.'

She looked so vulnerable standing there in the sunlight that Shane was about to put his arms around her and summon up the courage to finally kiss her, but Geraldine shivered and let go of his hand, running quickly back across the causeway onto dry land. He followed her, glancing across the Rock Road towards Sion Hill where another evening of tension awaited him. It soured his mood. The playfulness was gone from their afternoon. Shane realised how badly he wanted to kiss her, how he wanted some gesture that would cement their relationship.

'Let's go to the pool tomorrow,' he said. 'I'll teach you to swim.'

'You know I hate water.'

'Coward,' he teased.

'Don't say that.'

But he couldn't stop himself. 'Coward.'

Geraldine ignored him, walking ahead as they left the park in silence and took the muddy path by the train tracks that served as a short cut to Blackrock Station. It was so narrow that there was no way past when Shane saw the path ahead blocked by Simon Wallace, his surly teenage neighbour. Wallace was hunched down, with a naggin of whiskey in his hands. He looked up.

'What do we have here: two love-birds? Off for a snog, are you?'

'Don't be gross,' Geraldine said.

'Is this your drinking den?' Shane asked 'You said you drank somewhere you were never disturbed.'

'Well, I was wrong, wasn't I? Because I was disturbed there this afternoon. I just don't know if it was by the living or the dead.'

'What do you mean?'

'There's an old house at the end of Castledawson Avenue.'

'Yeah, I know it.'

Wallace looked at Shane sharply. 'What do you mean, you know it? You're only a wet weekend in Blackrock after escaping from the skangers in Sallynoggin.'

Shane made a movement towards him and Geraldine stepped between them.

'That's right, hide behind your girlfriend,' Wallace

sneered, but Shane noticed that the older boy had taken a precautionary step backwards. He wasn't just drunk, he was genuinely rattled. He also seemed to resent the fact that Shane had made a friend at last – especially a female one.

'I know that old house too,' Geraldine said. 'My gran says that two old brothers used to live there, with the house falling down around them. They both went mad and were found dead.'

'Anyone would go mad living there,' Wallace said. 'I set foot in the kitchen once and ran out when I felt the hairs on the back of my neck standing out. But I wouldn't even go back into the garden now.'

'Why not?'

'If you hop over the back wall it's like being in another world. I use the garden as a place to smoke a little weed in peace. But this afternoon I was scared witless. A candle appeared in the basement window. It's always dark in that basement because of the bushes around it. This gaunt geezer was staring out, with a long face like he was hundreds of years old. I didn't stick around to see if he was a ghost or not. I took one look and hopped back over the wall. A stray cat sitting up there scratched the arms off me.' He revealed two long scrapes down his forearm. 'I'm still shaking.'

'You probably just drank too much,' Shane said.

Wallace looked at him menacingly. 'If you want to call me a liar, then you break in there some evening and figure out who he is. Now, leave me alone before I give you a dig that will knock you back to Sallynoggin.'

Wallace raised the bottle to his lips, and they quickly walked past him towards the Dart station, only slowing down when they reached Idrone Terrace. They agreed he was telling lies to scare them because that house was too derelict for anybody to live there.

'Even standing outside it always gives me the creeps,' Shane admitted. 'I wouldn't set foot in it.'

Geraldine looked at him. 'So, who's the coward now?'

'This is different.'

'The only difference is that I could actually drown in a swimming pool. What can happen to you in an old house? How come it's OK for you to be scared of something, but not me?'

Geraldine's voice had a teasing quality, but Shane also felt that this was a test. 'I'll go in there,' he said, 'if you'll go with me.'

Geraldine looked away for a moment and then looked back and nodded.

'OK,' she agreed quietly. 'We can't always be afraid of things; it's not like we're kids any more.'

It felt as if Simon Wallace's story had set them a test of courage, a rite of passage. Undoubtedly, they would find nobody there, but with the summer almost ended, here at last might be the chance to investigate a genuine mystery.

TWELVE

Joey

November 2009

The mid-term exams were looming in Stradbrook College and I was getting a bit freaked out at the prospect. I was never anything more than an average student, but for Mum's sake I wanted to do well and show that her efforts to get me into Stradbrook had been worth it. The subject that most spooked me was history. I understood the general gist of it and even enjoyed those bits I could relate to. But memorising the dates of land acts and changes of government was beyond me. So when Shane offered to help me revise for our history exam, I was right up for going back to his lodgings after school.

I texted Mum and she texted back to say that this was fine once I didn't stay out too late. Then the battery on my phone died, as it often did. My phone was held together with sticky tape after numerous falls. Being put down the toilet in my old school hadn't helped it either. It had taken three weeks to dry out after that. Mum and I had become expert at reassembling its entrails – like open-heart surgeons as we nursed it through another few weeks. I knew that she was saving up to surprise me with a new phone on my birthday. I cursed the battery dying now but at least she knew where I was.

Shane's place was as he had described it, a granny flat attached to a house on Pine Lawn off Newtownpark Avenue. A flustered-looking woman appeared from the kitchen when Shane opened the front door. He introduced me to his landlady, Mrs Higgins, who said I was welcome to stay for dinner. I could see her young sons engrossed on an Xbox in the front room. She had two bedrooms upstairs let out to students studying art in Dún Laoghaire, girls in their early twenties with whom Shane had little contact. Mrs Higgins's house bustled with life, but Shane's room seemed detached from the bustle. When he closed the door his room felt colder and I had a sense of being cut off from everything. We lay on his bed and took out our history books. Soon there was a knock and Mrs Higgins brought in two dinners on a tray. When Shane went to wash his hands Mrs Higgins looked at me with open curiosity.

'You're the first friend Shane ever brought back,' she said. 'The first caller of any kind, for that matter.'

'I'm brutal at history,' I explained. 'He's giving me a hand for an exam.'

'He'd be the boy, all right: always at the history books or his computer whenever he's here. He wouldn't even put up a few posters on the walls. The only personal touch he put in the room is a set of Russian dolls.' She pointed at a shelf. 'You know, the dolls that you keep opening to find a smaller doll inside them. What class of hobby is that? Though he seems to spend most of his time on Internet gambling sites. Never says if he wins or loses, but I think he has the devil's own luck with money. Still, it's nice to see that at least he has one friend. Enjoy your dinner.'

The food was nice, but I wondered what it must feel like to eat all your meals on a tray. Shane was welcome to eat with the Higgins family but he disliked doing so because he felt in the way. He was allowed the use of Mrs Higgins's front room that was meant for both family and guests. But this was all he was – a guest. I wondered what it must be like to have only this converted garage to call your home.

But I soon forgot such thoughts because he had me in stitches, doing impersonations of teachers while we ate. Once we began to study, however, he grew serious. There seemed to be nothing about history that he didn't know and – better still – couldn't explain in simple terms. It was only when we finished studying that I began to take in his room again. It didn't feel like any teenager's bedroom: the walls were bare and almost monastic. The furniture was nice, but I could never have coped with living in space like this, like a prison cell. Shane seemed to sense my unease.

'This gaff is comfortable,' he said with such conviction that I didn't know which of us he was trying hardest to convince. 'I'm happy here.'

'But what do you do at night?' I asked. 'You don't even have a television in your room.'

'Mrs Higgins offered to buy me one but I said no. I have the Internet and my history books. This house backs onto the tennis club. Some nights I like to sit out in the garden in the dark when the tennis courts are closed and there's nobody around to disturb me.'

'That sounds a bit creepy.'

Shane grinned. 'It's just the calm before the storm, before I head into town and let it rip. I am a bit of a rake really, a gambler who can't resist a final bet.' He stood up. 'Grab your coat, we're hitting the road.'

'I have to get home to my mum,' I said. 'And anyway, my school bag weighs a ton.'

'Leave your bag here,' Shane insisted. 'I'll bring it in to-morrow. You studied hard; you need to relax hard.' He noticed my hesitation. 'Your mum was young once too, you know. Do you think she ran away home with her tail between her legs at eight o'clock every night, at your age? I bet she was out having a ball and she could still be having one now, because she's probably a fine-looking woman. There's nobody forcing her to sit at home like a spinster every night, making you feel guilty if you're not there to keep her company.'

'Leave my mum out of this,' I said, annoyed.

He laughed. 'I'm just saying that she could be a goer, if she wanted to.'

'Just shut up about my mum, all right.'

'I'm merely saying she should broaden her horizons, like you need to broaden yours. If you think this room is small, then it's time that you saw how other people live.' He picked up his leather jacket and stood in the doorway, waiting for me with an amused smile. 'So what's it to be – do you fancy a bit of hellfire or do you intend to run home scared to your mum all your life?'

THIRTEEN

Shane

August 2007

Geraldine and Shane met later that evening at the narrow entrance to Castledawson Avenue, a cul-de-sac that thousands of drivers sped past every day on the Rock Road without noticing. The noise of traffic faded as they walked up what was little more than a lane now, although a line of cottages had once stood on the right-hand side, where the playing fields of Blackrock College now lay empty in the summer twilight. Only two buildings remained standing on the left: old houses converted into smartly maintained offices. Both were overshadowed by the modern hospital complex of the Blackrock Clinic behind them. The lane grew narrower and petered out when they reached the deserted dairy.

Looking up at the chunks of masonry that had crumbled on the front wall, Shane and Geraldine felt certain that nobody could possibly live here. The front door had a brass door knocker but they had no intention of knocking. Investigators work in secret, though they were not really there to investigate. Shane saw this more as a chance to be alone with Geraldine. If she grew scared, it would be an excuse to put his arms around her. And if he found the courage to explore this empty house, then maybe he might find the courage to do what he had longed to do in Blackrock Park this afternoon and kiss her. One kiss would be sufficient to make his summer – which had begun in such loneliness – complete. He wondered if his grandparents had first kissed in this house, away from the prying disapproval of their employer. He had never known his grandmother and it was hard to imagine his grandfather ever being so young. Shane looked at Geraldine.

'Do you want to go back?'

Geraldine returned his look. 'Don't tell me you're too much of a wimp to prove that boy a liar?'

Shane didn't know if the glint in her eye was meant as a tease or a dare, but it was enough to ensure that he would not back down now. He would explore every room in this house until it was Geraldine who begged him to turn back. A tiny path ran along by the side wall and ended at a rusted iron gate with barbed wire on top. This gate was impossible to scale but some stones had tumbled down from the wall, leaving enough footholds for them to climb it. An old black cat, a half-wild stray sitting at the far end of the wall, observed them unblinkingly. From the top of the wall they could see the grounds of Blackrock College on one side and the car park of the Blackrock Clinic on the other, but when they jumped down into the garden itself they could see nothing except a jungle of sky-high brambles and bushes that covered the slope which led down towards the basement of the old house.

Empty flagons were scattered around the bushes, along

with smashed bottles of spirits and cigarette butts. But all this rubbish was in a corner right beside the gate. It was as if even the people who held illicit drinking parties here had kept their distance from the house. Shane hoped that Geraldine would lose her nerve, but it was she who led the way, hacking a path through towering clusters of nettles. Finally a gap appeared amid the bushes and they raced down the rest of the slope, only able to stop when their outstretched hands slammed against the basement wall, with loose pebbledash crumbling beneath their fingers.

The kitchen windows looked dark, as branches pressed against them. The glass panes were spider-webbed with such long cracks that they resembled secret maps. Catching his breath and nursing his scratched arms, Shane gazed in through the windows at the basement where his grandfather had worked as a boy. It looked forboding in the twilight. The Rock Road was only a hundred yards away, but as Shane looked back up at the tangle of bushes they had pushed their way through, it felt as if they had entered a timeless place.

Then, through the silence, he heard a sound that chilled him: a distant drip, as if a falling droplet of water had rippled a still surface. He looked at Geraldine, but she seemed to hear nothing. If Shane was alone he might have turned back. But he wasn't going to let Geraldine away with calling him a wimp. Geraldine looked scared too, but she was equally determined not to be the one who backed down. Gazing into this dark kitchen unnerved her, however, and she knew that unless she acted immediately she would be too paralysed with terror to continue.

'Lift me up,' Geraldine whispered, pointing to a small window that was slightly ajar. 'I bet I can squeeze through.'

'Are you sure you want to?' Shane asked.

'You're an awful scaredy-cat, do you know that?'

Shane bent down to lift her up. Inch by inch, the iron frame opened, with her fingers turning brown from the stardust of rust. There was a cloying stench of stale air when she put her head through the window. Geraldine was halfway inside now. She felt a sudden terror that if she fell forward and sprained her ankle, she might not be able to get back out. She wanted to tell Shane to lift her down, but when she turned her head to speak she was overcome by a sensation of being swept forward against her will by an invisible torrent of water. She put her arms out in fright and lost her balance, falling through the window and landing on the kitchen floor. It was bone dry and the sensation of drowning was gone. But she felt so breathless that she could not answer Shane's frantic calls. He immediately scrambled his way in through the window, concerned only for Geraldine. He cut his elbow on the frame, and she heard him wince as he landed beside her.

'Are you OK, Shane?'

'Never mind me – what happened to you?'

They could barely see each other in the gloom. Any light entering the kitchen was tinged in green because of the tangled vegetation growing against the window. Shane switched on his torch, startling her with its strong beam.

She had wanted Shane to enter this house with her as a test of his courage, but just now she longed to be back home. The torch beam picked out a small door at the far end of the kitchen. Shane rose to open it and shine his torch into a narrow passageway that sloped sharply down towards what looked like an empty cellar. Again he heard the drip of a solitary drop of water, the sound amplified by the narrow walls. The coldness of that passageway scared him. He slammed the door shut. Geraldine gasped as the noise echoed through the basement. 'Do you think anyone heard?'

'I don't know,' he whispered. Both of them had the sense that they were not alone here, but did not wish to scare the other by talking of ghosts. 'Drug dealers could be using this place as a base,' he added, not believing this himself but needing to find some concrete reason to explain his sense of fear of being overheard. 'We'd better keep our voices down.'

He switched off the torch and Geraldine gripped his hand because the kitchen seemed so much darker without it. Both of them glanced back at the window. They were scared but neither wanted to climb back through the window just yet. Reluctantly, they left the kitchen and entered a corridor paved with large flagstones. A mouse scurried past and Geraldine suppressed a scream. She wondered what other creatures had made their homes in these rooms. Shane switched back on his torch, covering the beam with his fingers so that only thin shafts of light filtered through. It was enough for them to see that there were no stolen goods or stashed drugs in this corridor; no cigarette butts or dusty footprints or other clues that criminals were meant to leave behind. The only sign of life came from huge spiders in the thick cobwebs that brushed against their heads, leaving Geraldine terrified that a spider might get tangled up in her hair.

They reached the start of a flight of stairs leading up to the main hallway. Both felt less scared now and became convinced that Simon Wallace was lying, because it seemed obvious that nobody had entered this house in years. Still, the further they explored, the further they were going away from the small window that was their only escape route.

'My grandad once worked here,' Shane told Geraldine quietly. 'This is where he met his wife-to-be when they were our age.'

'You're making that up.'

'No, it's true. He once told me that they had their first kiss sitting at the top of these stairs.'

Shane had invented the last bit, but Geraldine looked at him strangely and then walked up into the darkness to sit on the top step and stare back down at him. He knew that she was waiting for him to follow and realised that she had been waiting for weeks for him to kiss her. He walked slowly up each step, trying to look cool but knowing that he was failing miserably. When he reached her, she made space on the top step. They both peered around at the hallway, lit by a dim gleam of light through the fanlight above the locked front door. A dilapidated staircase led to the bedrooms on the first floor. Shane shivered – not just from the cold and dark, but also be-

cause of the odd sensation that he had been here before
in a dream. Geraldine was smiling at him.

'Maybe you're not such a wimp after all,' she said.

'We can say that the first and last case in our investiga-
tion agency is solved and officially closed.'

'It's S. W. A. L. K.'

'What does that mean?'

Geraldine laughed. 'Why are boys so stupid? You don't
know anything. It means "Sealed With A Loving Kiss".'

Geraldine stopped laughing then because her eyes were
serious. She and Shane had earned this moment. Maybe
they had not explored the entire house, but they had
proved themselves far braver than Simon Wallace. They
could enjoy their first kiss and maybe their second and
third, and after they were finished could walk hand in
hand back down to the kitchen and leave, laughing as they
raced down the Rock Road like a real couple at last. Shane
leaned forward and just as their lips were about to touch
they heard it: a faint crackling hiss of jazz coming from
somewhere inside the house.

The music dissolved into a quiet babble of static, as if
someone was searching for a clearer radio signal. Then the
tune resumed, clearer now – with a haunting clarinet. All
thoughts of kissing were abandoned. They longed to flee,
but Shane seemed hypnotised by that music. It made no
sense, but he had the notion that if he opened a door he
might glimpse the young ghosts of his grandparents
dancing slowly to the tune.

Geraldine hissed at him to come back but he ignored
her as he crept across the bare floorboards in the hallway.

Rather then be left alone, she followed him past the main staircase and down a side passageway towards where a door was open just a crack. Light came from within this room, so faint that they had not seen it previously. Some-one was in there.

Shane stopped in the doorway, mesmerised by the light and the music. Geraldine joined him and they peered through a tiny gap in the open doorway. The room contained no stash of stolen banknotes or slabs of heroin, just an old man hunched over an ancient radio. The flames from two candles wedged into bottles were so faint that no trace of light filtered through the tattered blankets that he had placed across the window so as not to betray his presence to the outside world. They stared in at his few possessions: a small pile of books, a tiny gas stove and a saucepan, a sleeping bag on an old mattress, two jars of pills, a battered armchair, a half-finished loaf of bread, a coffee jar and a few cracked plates and cups.

The old man had his back to them, trying to get the radio signal as clear as possible. Then he stood up and, throwing back his head, began to dance, almost as if in slow motion. He laughed as he twirled round. For a minute his ancient limbs seemed to defy time and almost defy gravity. Then he stumbled and fell backwards, startling Shane and Geraldine who were too scared to move. From the way that he landed, utterly still with his head thrown back and his eyes closed, they could not tell if he was alive or dead.

FOURTEEN

Joey

November 2009

After we left Mrs Higgins's house, Shane and I got a 46A bus into Dublin. Because my phone battery was dead, I was unable to call Mum about my change of plans and I had felt shy about asking Mrs Higgins for permission to use her phone. Shane was the only student I knew who refused to carry a mobile. By the time we reached O'Connell Street, the main shops were closed, with only amusement arcades and fast food restaurants open. You needed to mind yourself at this hour. Rooting in your pockets for change or simply looking lost could lead to an unprovoked attack.

A gang was gathered under the portico of the General Post Office. They ranged in age from twelve to eighteen and all looked foreign: African, Asian and Eastern European. They stopped talking to watch us approach. My survival skills had taught me to avoid eye contact in these situations, to make myself as invisible as possible. I didn't like their menacing silence, but if we could just manage to walk another few feet beyond them, the danger point would be passed.

However, as we reached them, Shane deliberately

shouldered the tallest black youth, knocking him back into the others. The youth angrily straightened up and pushed Shane. Suddenly we were surrounded by a mêlée of foreign faces. Yet I might not have existed. Their focus was exclusively on Shane. He kept shoving people aggressively. His movements, his attitude, his half-mumbled jibes to insult them reminded me of a gangsta rapper. The youths responded with equal aggression: there was a tense vibe in the air. Passers-by gave us a wide berth, anxious to avoid getting caught up in what seemed like an ugly row. Shane used his elbows to clear enough space to raise his fists in a boxing stance. Crouching, he said something in a foreign tongue that caused the muscular youth towering over him to throw back his head and laugh. This started off the others laughing too, and amidst their shared hilarity I suddenly saw them differently – not as a dangerous gang, but a group of pals play-acting, squaring up to each other in jest. Shane put his arm around my shoulders.

'This, gentlemen, is my mate Joey Kilmichael, songwriter and guitarist extraordinaire. Joey, meet the guys.'

I shook hands as Shane introduced them. But it was impossible to keep track of their names or their country of origin. At first I thought they had nothing in common, but after a while I realised that they were linked by the fact of no longer possessing any family. They were child refugees who had reached Ireland alone. At some stage, parents in Zaire or Somalia had realised that, while their entire family had little chance of asylum, no Western government could turn its back on a solitary child washed up on their shores. All seemed to have reached Ireland by sea.

Some remembered their parents paying couriers who locked them into dark containers loaded into the hold of ships and others claimed to remember nothing, perhaps because their parents had warned them that the safest way to survive was to forget, that if you had no identity there was nowhere to which you could be sent back.

The Irish government made sure that they were fed and clothed, had schools to attend and a room in a hostel. But there was a difference between a room and a home, which was why they sought each other out at night. I re-alised, too, why Shane looked so relaxed among them. Of course he was no refugee and would collect an inheritance on his twenty-first birthday. But, like them, if he woke from a nightmare at night there was no one to whom he could turn for comfort.

As we walked down Henry Street I felt out of my depth. Some lads spoke good English, but others knew only a few words or had accents that I could not make out. Bouncers outside amusement arcades eyed us warily. We reached the huge cinema complex on Parnell Street, its steps thronged with cinema-goers. Few of us had the price of a cinema ticket and, even if we had, I suspected that we could never have agreed on one choice.

The youngest boy, Niyi, sat on the steps and silently listened to music on his MP3 player while the others stood talking in a babble of tongues. He was with the group yet seemed utterly apart in his private world. I sat beside him because I also felt lost. Niyi ignored me at first, then removed the tiny earphones and silently handed me one earpiece. He replaced the other one in his own ear. I followed suit so that we could share the rap music blasting out at full volume.

A security guard emerged from the plate glass doors to move us along. The others reluctantly moved off, shouting back at the guard. Niyi rose and I rose too. Our heads close together, our fingers keeping the earphones in place, we followed the group onto Capel Street. The song ended and the boy removed his earphone. I did likewise and handed mine back to him. He accepted it silently, making no attempt to catch up with the others. Music blasted from a pub on a corner, where girls queued to get past the bouncers. My mother would be worried that I was not home by now. Down a side street I could see a music shop with an expensive-looking blue guitar occupying pride of place in the window. I wanted to pause and admire it, but Niyi had already moved on, anxious to keep the others in sight. I caught up with him and he broke his silence.

'So, he found you too.'

'Who?'

'Shane.'

'What do you mean by found?' I asked.

'Before he finds me I never go out after dark. Too scared. I know no one and it is always cold here. Even Irish people are cold behind their smiles. My mother warned me; be careful.'

'Of what?'

'Of everything.'

'Where is your mother now?'

He looked at me with sudden hostility. 'You a policeman?'

'No. I was just asking.'

'Don't ask.'

We walked on in silence then, because I didn't know
what to say. Ahead of us, the other lads were shouldering
each other and scrambling to kick an empty can. Shane
was laughing in their midst. I had never before considered
what it must be like to feel buried alive in a sealed con-
tainer in the dark hold of a ship, never certain if you
would see daylight again and then to emerge halfway
across the world, knowing absolutely no one. I had read
reports of such voyages in newspapers, but something
about Niyi's manner told me that I had yet to earn the
right to ask him what his own journey in Ireland had been
like.

'Sorry for the stupid questions,' I said.

He shrugged. 'You OK.'

'How do you know Shane?'

'He knocks at my door in Dún Laoghaire one night. I
am lying on bed listening to music. Nobody ever knocks
on my door so I ignore him, but he refuse to go away until
I answer. Shane is standing there, grinning. "Come on
out," he says, "you can't stay in every night." "Who the
hell you be?" I ask. "What the hell you want? Where the
hell you come from?" He just keeps smiling, saying, "Let's
go, let's smell the sea air." At first he scare me – I think he
want something, you know – but he just good guy. Bit
crazy, but good. Through him I meet the other guys.'

'Are they good guys?'

'They OK. They give me something to do at night so I no longer feel always alone. But I never know how Shane knocks at my door. The only other people who knock are social workers, always asking questions.'

The others had reached the quays and were waiting to cross onto Capel Street Bridge. Good-natured taunts were being exchanged with three teenage girls beside them, dolled up for a night out in impossibly short black cocktail dresses. Traffic was heavy. If the lights changed, the others would get across the bridge before us and we might lose them.

'Do you want to catch up with your friends?' I asked.

'They are not friends. Only Shane is my friend.'

A gap appeared in the traffic and the teenage girls decided to risk crossing the road. They raced out with mock shrieks. Despite the blaring car horns there was no real danger until one girl, lagging behind her friends, slipped in her high heels. She managed to stand back up, but looked startled by the lights of the oncoming car. The driver tried to stop. He slammed on the brakes but slammed into her as well, throwing her body into the air. She hit the windscreen and bounced off. There was absolute stillness for a moment: the girl lay still with one high heel on and another a few yards away. The traffic was halted and it almost seemed as if life had stopped. Then the road was filled with people as the girl's friends started to scream.

The driver emerged from his car and hunched down, shaking. When I reached the middle of the road a circle had formed. The girl's friends were hysterical. People didn't know what to do. When Shane stepped forward nobody stopped him because he was possessed of a quiet authority. He knelt beside the girl and felt her pulse. Then he leaned forward and pressed his lips close to her ear. The murmur of shocked voices was growing, but I could plainly hear the words that Shane was whispering. I could not understand them because they were in Latin, but I knew that he was solemnly praying for her departed soul. Everyone present seemed to recognise this, because they fell silent and, when he finished and stood up, many people instinctively blessed themselves.

There were sirens in the distance now. A motorcycle cop appeared and took command of the situation. As he waved aside a line of cars to let the ambulance through, people's attention shifted from Shane. The other boys were anxious to get away – sharing the anxiety which all outsiders feel that, somehow, they might be held to blame. It was the first time I had ever seen anyone die. I was shaking. I wanted my mother to be there to hold me. We crossed the bridge in silence and on the south quays we gathered around a sculpture in the shape of a Viking boat. We were all shocked. Lads slipped away until there was just Shane and me and Niyi, who was listening to his music and saying nothing. Shane touched his shoulder, and when Niyi removed his earphones and looked up, I saw that he was crying.

'Get the last DART back to Dún Laoghaire,' Shane said softly. 'Things will be okay. Trust me.'

'Why should I trust anyone?' The boy turned to go and then paused. 'I do trust you,' he said quietly. 'Promise you will call.'

Shane nodded and I watched Niyi walk away, his shoulders hunched.

'How did you find Niyi?' I asked.

Shane shrugged. 'He was a shipwrecked sailor. That's what they all are.'

'And what are you then?'

'Think of me as being like a beachcomber. Folks in Blackrock eked out a living that way for centuries, you know, combing the rocks for timber or washed-up bales of silk or shipwrecked bodies to plunder after storms. I am more like a soul-comber though: I comb for washed-up souls.'

'What the hell does that mean?'

Shane looked at me for a moment as if about to say something and then just laughed. 'It means nothing; it's nonsense, like when Eric Cantona talked about the seagulls following the trawler. I'm having a laugh with you.'

'Really? And so tell me, where did you learn those Latin prayers you whispered into that girl's ear?'

Shane shrugged, amused. 'What makes you think I know Latin? Maybe I know the odd phrase. When I was small I wanted to be a priest. It's amazing the bits you pick up as an altar server at Mass.'

'Shane, priests haven't said Mass in Latin for donkey's years.'

Shane raised his eyes to heaven. 'How come you know

shag all about history, but you're suddenly an expert on religion? Come on, let's go.'

'Are we getting the last bus home?'

'You disappoint me, Joey. A girl just died before your eyes and all you can think about is going home?'

Shane turned and, as he did so, he appeared to stumble because he fell backwards. From the way he landed with his head thrown back and his eyes closed, I was scared that he had cracked his skull on the pavement. But as I leaned forward anxiously his eyes opened mischievously and he clicked his fingers. 'Life can be snatched away like this,' he said. 'Surely that should make even a dormouse like you want to take the odd risk? So, are you a wimp or a rake?'

Springing to his feet, Shane strode off along the quays, not bothering to look back. He was setting me a test and waiting to see if I would follow.

FIFTEEN

Shane

August 2007

For several moments, Geraldine and Shane stared at the old man sprawled on the floor. Then his eyes opened, almost mischievously, as if he had been setting them a test. Observing them upside-down, he swept out one arm in a wry gesture of welcome and murmured something in a tongue that neither of them understood. He saw their confused looks and smiled. 'My Latin is rusty,' he said. 'It translates as, "Step into my parlour, said the spider to the fly." '

Shane wanted to run, but his feet seemed turned to stone. It was Geraldine who stepped forward.

'What are you doing here?' she demanded, trying to make herself sound older.

'What am I doing here?' The old man didn't try to stand up. But he seemed in no pain. 'As it happens, I live here. This is my house. I was born here. So, could I ask you the same question? What are you doing here?'

'We didn't know anyone lived here,' Geraldine replied.

'So why did you come?'

'We were just messing around,' Shane said. 'We'd formed a sort of club.'

'What type of club?'

'To investigate mysteries.'

Shane realised how foolish the notion seemed, but he could think of nothing else that would explain their presence. However, the old man seemed to treat the idea seriously. 'And have you solved any?' he asked, slowly getting to his feet.

'No,' Geraldine confessed. 'You were our first case.'

'Who sent you here?' The man's voice hardened.

'Nobody,' Shane insisted.

'Are you sure?' His eyes looked suddenly manic. 'How do you know they are not using you?'

'Who are you talking about?'

'When you finish investigating me, who do you report back to?'

'Nobody,' Geraldine interrupted, unnerved by the new tension in the room. 'It's a bit of fun. Besides, we don't know what you've done yet.'

'No, you don't.' He laughed, but there was a frightening loneliness in that laugh. 'That's one dark mystery all right.'

Geraldine looked around the bare room and shivered. The old man lowered himself into the armchair. 'I'm sorry.' He smiled apologetically. 'It's unfair of me to scare you like that.'

'We're not scared,' Geraldine said, but both she and Shane edged towards the door.

'I'm just not used to visitors,' the old man said. 'I guard my privacy. I'm only getting used to being home again.'

'Is this really your home?' Shane asked. He realised that

the old man was studying his face intensely. 'What are you staring at?' he said, disturbed.

'It feels like I'm staring at an old friend.'

'I don't know you.'

'It's not you I know; it's your face: I've seen your face before. Yes, this is indeed my home, but it has lain empty for years. Maybe you two have been here before?'

'We were never here,' Geraldine said quickly. 'A boy told us he saw something through the window this afternoon.'

The old man nodded. 'I did spy a figure stumbling around the garden, but I knew they hadn't sent him: he would be too weak to be of use to them.'

'What are you talking about?' Shane asked, puzzled. 'And how could you possibly know my face?'

'Your face will come to me,' the old man said. 'Faces always do. I can't stop them floating through my mind. I was careless to let myself be glimpsed, but I didn't think that young man had seen me or would remember, because life gets blurred through the end of a whiskey bottle. I speak as the black sheep of a once respectable Blackrock family.'

'Did your two brothers live here?' Geraldine asked.

'Yes,' the man replied. 'They shared the one roof all their lives, yet for their final thirty years, neither spoke to the other. They now share a grave with my mother.'

'People say this house is haunted,' Geraldine said.

The man smiled. 'Do you believe in ghosts?'

'No.' But Geraldine couldn't stop an involuntary shiver. 'Not in daylight anyway.'

'At night you're not so sure?'

'You're not a ghost, are you?'

The old man laughed. 'My name is Thomas McCormack. I've never even seen a ghost, though I often slept in graveyards when I was homeless in America.'

'Were you a hobo?' Shane asked.

The man smiled. 'I suppose so. I suppose we're all hobos until God claims our souls. For decades I lived among the homeless and the confused and drug addicts and drunks and, if they asked me, I'd hear their confessions and whisper the last rites in Latin as they lay dying.'

'Are you a priest then?' Geraldine enquired.

'No. Though when I left this house to study for the priesthood, the neighbours genuflected as they gathered to say goodbye. I was a right swank back then, someone the whole neighbourhood looked up to.'

'What happened?' Shane asked.

'Sometimes you need to leave home to find out who you really are,' the old man replied. 'Somebody told me a long time ago that dozens of personalities lurk inside each of us – good and evil – waiting for their chance to get out. They have all got their chance with me over the decades. Does that answer your question, young Master O'Driscoll?'

'I never told you my name,' Shane said, scared now.

'I said I would place your face, though it took me a moment because you also have a touch of the O'Learys in your features.'

'O'Leary was my grandmother's name.'

'And was she from Blackrock?'

'Yes. So was my grandfather.'

'And he was an O'Driscoll?'

Shane felt excited and uneasy. 'That's right.'

'And where did they first meet?'

'Slaving for a cranky woman under this very roof.'

Thomas McCormack nodded. 'My mother had a sharp tongue, God rest her soul. And your grandmother had a marvellous laugh if her name was Molly. Was her name Molly?'

'How do you know this?'

'Your grandad, Jack, used to call her Mollser, or at least he did when he was your age.'

A memory returned to Shane of his grandfather drifting in and out of consciousness on his deathbed and suddenly saying this pet name as if his late wife had just appeared beside his hospital bed.

'I only ever heard Grandad use that name once.' Shane said, blinking back unexpected tears.

The old man smiled. 'If you had visited this house seventy years ago you would have heard it a lot more. She was a great dancer, your grandmother. I remember dancing with Molly to a jazz record in this room, with your grandad keeping watch for fear that my mother would find us. My mother would have sacked Molly on the spot for dancing to the devil's music. She would have been furious at me for being over-familiar with a servant, especially when a boy destined for the priesthood was not meant to be interested in dancing. I was a lousy dancer, mind you. The real dancing only happened when Molly and Jack would glide around this room and I took my turn to keep watch at the door.'

Glancing around the desolate room with its mildew-stained walls, Shane found himself imagining the scene. 'I can't believe you knew my grandad,' he said.

Thomas McCormack leaned forward, his voice so low that Shane could hardly hear it. 'I know your grandfather and your great-grandfather; I know all the O'Driscolls going right back to when Blackrock was known as New-town-at-the-Black-Rock. We're old neighbours, you and I; we go back centuries. That worries me. Maybe they led you here or maybe you came by chance, but do yourself a favour, young O'Driscoll. Forget we ever met. When I slipped unnoticed into this house some weeks ago my aim was to stay unnoticed.'

'Who are you in hiding from?' Geraldine asked.

The old man turned, slightly startled, as if he had momentarily forgotten that she was in the room. 'There's a touch of the Flemings in your face,' he said. 'The Flemings were always great swimmers. Are you a Fleming?'

'I want to go now,' Geraldine said, sharply. 'Shane, let's go.'

'Yes, that would be wise.' The old man winced suddenly and held his chest. 'Just pass me those blue tablets first, the painkillers there.'

Geraldine handed him the tablets, alarmed at the pain clearly visible on his face. 'Who's looking after you?' she said. 'Does a doctor know you're living here?'

He swallowed two tablets, washed down with water

from a cup on the table. 'Not a living soul knows, except the solicitor who tracked me down in America. You might say that you're my only friends.'

Shane and Geraldine exchanged an uneasy glance.

'Friend is too strong a word,' the old man added, 'but you now have the power to betray my secret.'

'What secret?'

'I never expected to see my home again. I planned to disturb no one, but unfortunately you disturbed me. You see, I'm here on a secret mission.'

'What mission?' Shane asked.

The old man smiled. 'If I told you, it wouldn't be a secret any more. I'll tell you if you make me a member of your club. Then it will be an official club secret. I was a member of a club once before, high up in the Dublin mountains.'

'We don't really have a club, even though we do have a password,' Geraldine said. 'We're only having a laugh, but not just anyone can join.'

'I'm not just anyone. You can help me with my mission.'

'How?'

'Are we sworn to secrecy?' Thomas asked.

Geraldine wanted to say that they could make no promises, but Shane nodded before she could speak.

'Your secret is safe with us, Thomas.'

Thomas gazed at Geraldine until she reluctantly nodded too.

'Your task is easy,' Thomas said, 'My task is more

difficult. Your job is to tell nobody what you saw tonight. Forget I ever existed. This house is my sanctuary. I need to do something here that I can only do on my own, something that I have put off for far too long. You have no need to ever return. But I want nobody else to disturb me. So please, don't tell a soul. Fate has brought me back to Blackrock one last time as a dying man. My mission is to finally end my life under the roof where I was born.' Thomas McCormack reached across to raise the volume of the jazz music that was playing and stared into Shane O'Driscoll's young face. 'I want to die alone here, unnoticed and truly unmourned.'

SIXTEEN

Joey

November 2009

I walked quickly along the quay wall to catch up with Shane. 'Where the hell are we going?' I asked.

'To a special gig,' he replied.

'At this time of night? Are you serious?'

'I'm always serious.'

'Shane, I have to get the last DART home. My mum will be …'

Shane stopped beside a parked car on the dimly-lit quay. The driver's window was smashed. Somebody had ripped out the CD player. He reached through the smashed window to pop up the button that unlocked the doors. Slipping into the driver's seat, he motioned for me to open the passenger door.

'What are you doing, Shane?' I hissed.

'I'm bringing you to your gig in style.'

'I just want to go home.'

'You'll get home; now just get into the car first. You're making us look suspicious.'

It was true. I was being picked up in the headlights of all the passing cars as I stood there with the door ajar. Reluctantly, I sat in beside him. 'Shane, can you even drive?'

'The hardest part of driving is simply getting the car started. That's why you need an old banger like this without central locking.' He pulled out wires from under the dash and joined them together. The engine came to life with a roar. 'The second hardest part, of course, is getting the damn car to stop.'

'Shane, let me out.'

But it was too late. Shane pulled out, to the consternation of the driver behind us who beeped violently. Shane swung right, breaking a red light at the next bridge, and brought us back across the river, turning down a warren of side streets littered with smashed pallets outside deserted fruit warehouses.

'You're raving mad, Shane. Stop this car.'

'I will … in time. Don't worry.'

He swung right so that we were suddenly going the wrong way up a one-way system towards the junction with Capel Street. Cars were still backed up there because of the accident on the quays. Shane did not slow down, although there was barely space for us to squeeze through the jam of vehicles. We sped onto another side street and were passing the music shop with the blue guitar in the window when Shane braked violently. I looked behind, shaking but relieved that he had stopped. If he reversed back, there was just enough space to park the car outside the music shop. Shane followed my gaze.

'I bet you noticed that guitar when we were walking down.'

'It's a beauty all right,' I agreed. 'Now let's ditch this car.'

Only then did I realise what Shane intended to do. He reversed between the parked vehicles but made no attempt to straighten up. Instead he mounted the footpath and crashed the car boot into the shop window. It shattered into a thousand pieces, with shards of glass raining down. The guitar was undamaged, still sitting there. I could not believe this was happening. It felt like something from a film. Shane laughed at my shocked face.

'I go to all this effort and you just sit there, Joey,' he said. 'At least have the decency to jump out and grab that guitar.'

Again, it felt like a test, and again, I did as instructed because at that moment nothing felt real. It didn't feel like me reaching in through that window, or at least like any version of me I had previously known. It was like a glimpse into another world without rules. The alarm set off by the smashed window was ear-shatteringly loud. Outside the pub on the corner of Capel Street, the bouncers were speaking into walkie-talkies. At any moment the police could arrive. I knew that what we were doing was totally wrong, yet I let myself get carried along by Shane's madness. I threw the guitar into the back seat and barely managed to climb back into the car before Shane sped off with my door only half closed. A truck was approaching. We were directly in its path and seemed bound to crash but at the last second Shane turned up a pedestrianised street. He made an illegal left turn so that we were driving back up towards the cinema complex on Parnell Street. It was only half an hour since I had sat on the steps there with Niyi, but it felt like an age ago. During that time a girl had died, a car had been hot-wired, a shop window rammed, a guitar stolen. Yet I couldn't stop laughing, because Shane was laughing too. He swung right at the cinema and up Parnell Street, with both of us punching the roof and Shane shouting at the top of his voice, 'Spur up the horses. Make haste to the Eagle Tavern and the Hellfire Club! This is what it feels like to truly be alive!'

'To the Eagle Tavern!' I shouted back, and then the exhilaration left me as I realised the consequences of what we had just done. I wanted to ask him where the hell the Eagle Tavern was, but I said nothing because I felt sick and tricked by Shane. Most of all, I felt scared. I looked across at him, wondering how this could be the same boy who had helped me to study history in his room just a few hours ago. The boy who had actually looked too scared to enter the ruins of the Hellfire Club on our school retreat. What if he killed someone at this speed? I was out of my depth here, and had no idea where we were going. No wonder Geraldine had tried to warn me about him. Shane seemed to be in a world of his own as he navigated a maze of streets that brought us further and further into the north side. I knew the north side of Dublin – I just didn't know it personally. I was no snob. I knew its reputation was probably undeserved, but crashing a stolen car at midnight down some street off the North Strand certainly wasn't the best way to get acquainted with it.

'Stop the car,' I demanded. 'Shane, stop the damn car.'

He glanced across at me and smiled. 'I don't know

what you're worried about, we can't go much further. This heap of junk is nearly out of petrol.'

'I want to go home, Shane.'

'Sometimes you need to leave home to find out who you really are. Now just sit tight till I park this yoke where nobody will find it until morning. And fasten your seat belt. I can't always be minding you.'

We passed some blocks of flats and old red brick terraces. There was a large park to our right and a railway bridge ahead of us. After that, we were out onto the coast road at what I reckoned was Clontarf. Traffic was light, and there was nobody about except the odd person walking their dog. I could see across the water to the Poolbeg lights and then my view was interrupted by the shape of an island close to the shore.

It was Bull Island, a nature sanctuary formed by the slow build-up of sediment against the harbour wall. A wooden bridge led out to that wilderness. We were almost past the bridge when Shane swung onto it and accelerated, speeding across the narrow planks. The tide was out, with a thick expanse of mud on either side of us. Nobody lived on this wilderness of sand dunes, with meandering paths through its wild grass. Shane was pushing the engine to its limit, the car bouncing on the old planks. If we met a vehicle coming the other way we would not be able to stop. Maybe Shane didn't want to stop. Maybe he intended to kill us both out here in the darkness, away from the necklace of lights on the Clontarf Road that were growing ever more distant in the rear-view mirror.

'For God's sake, slow down,' I shouted.

Shane chuckled. 'I am more acquainted with the devil, but for your sake I'll stop. Now hold tight!'

We were now approaching the old concrete pier that stretched out into Dublin Bay. For a moment I thought that Shane planned to keep going across those rough stones, but then he turned violently left so that the car shot down a slope and we were driving on sand. The wheels sank down and got stuck and the car swung around. We came to a sudden halt, facing back the way that we had come. It took only a few seconds for the car to stop, but those seconds seemed to stretch into an eternity as I thought of the crash in which my father had died. I tried to catch my breath, unsure of whether I wanted to assault Shane or open the car door and run for my life. But when I looked across at Shane, he was laughing.

'That's what I call being alive,' he said. 'Can you feel the buzz? Can you feel it in your veins?'

'We could have been killed, you moron.'

'Stick with me, kid, and you'll never die.' Shane opened the driver's door. 'Let's go.'

'Where?'

'Just follow me, all right? A bit of trust wouldn't go astray here.'

'You're insane, Shane; do you know that?'

'Grab that guitar. We went to enough trouble stealing it. Now come on, there's a view I want to show you.'

SEVENTEEN

Thomas

August 1932

Thomas McCormack reaches across to raise the volume of the jazz music and stares into Jack O'Driscoll's young face. 'Sweep Molly up in your arms while you have the chance,' he says, 'Let's risk another spin around the floor before my mother comes back.'

He watches the servant boy whirl the teenage maid across the room with vibrant, laughing steps. Molly and Jack are making up the dance as they go along, thrilled to be holding each other, thrilled at the illicit feel of dancing when they are meant to be scrubbing and slaving for their fearsome employer. But every corner of this house already gleams so much, the lace curtains brilliantly white, the rooms so spick and span that Thomas doesn't know what is left for the servants to clean. However his mother rules the family home with such an iron fist that fourteen-year-old Thomas keeps a careful watch at the window for her return from the Blueshirts rally in Blackrock Town Hall.

His mother doesn't know that he possesses this sinful jazz record. He acquired it yesterday on his visit to old Dr Thomson, where he had lovingly examined all the foreign place names printed in gold leaf on the doctor's radiogram. The doctor had surprised the boy by placing this jazz record on his gramophone. Thomas had been unsure whether to listen because the priests in his school regularly denounced jazz as the devil's music. But the doctor had only laughed when Thomas said this and talked instead about changelings and Russian dolls and dangers to the soul, stuff that Thomas had not been able to follow.

The lure of the jazz record had proven hard to resist, because ever since his mother left the house today Thomas has been taking turns with Jack O'Driscoll to dance with the kitchen maid.

The record ends again and Jack steps away from Molly with a mock bow. He turns to Thomas. 'We may as well be hung for a sheep as a lamb,' he says. 'Have one last dance; I'll keep watch.' Molly is laughing, her face flushed with excitement as Thomas links his hands with hers and the music starts again.

'I could dance forever to this,' she says. 'I'd happily still be dancing here in this room in seventy years' time.'

Thomas swirls her around, knowing that he is not half as good a dancer as Jack O'Driscoll. Being servants, Jack and Molly are his social inferiors, but Thomas feels closer to them than he feels to his two older brothers. His eldest brother, Frank, has a confident adult stride as he patrols the yard each morning. Frank is the master-in-waiting who will inherit this house. The middle brother, Pete, is a harder worker, but – being a year younger than Frank – will forever be condemned to work for his elder sibling, trapped in the limbo of being neither a servant nor a man of property.

But it is their mother who dominates the dairy, and everyone was expected to know their place. Thomas's place is not to be dancing with servants but on his knees praying. He was four years old when his father's body was washed up on the shoreline – an incurable alcoholic said to have lost his footing when stumbling home drunk. Some neighbours darkly whispered about suicide, because he was mocked in the taverns of Blackrock and Kingstown for letting his wife wear the trousers. But at his funeral, the priest had predicted that his youngest son would be ordained and bring new souls to God in the foreign missions. His mother had clung onto this notion ever since, knowing that Thomas's vocation would banish any scandal about his father's death and bring the family great respectability and status in the neighbourhood.

Thomas twirls Molly around the room now. He loves the feel of her in his arms, but what is the point of liking a girl when everyone knows that he is destined to be a priest? Besides, it is obvious that Molly only has eyes for Jack.

'Is there any sign of the mistress?' Molly calls out to Jack and then whispers to Thomas, 'No offence, but your mother is the scariest person in the world.'

'I know someone scarier.'

'Who?'

'Old Joseph, who works for the nuns in Sion Hill.'

Molly shivers in his arms at the thought of the hunchback who arrives at the dairy every morning to collect milk for the convent in a donkey-cart. Joseph has slaved for the nuns for longer than anyone can remember, doing odd jobs and running their piggery. Jack laughs at the window.

'Old Joseph is harmless,' Jack says, 'he's just astray in the head.'

Thomas knows that the crippled mute is what his mother calls 'an incurable idiot'. But every morning when Joseph enters the yard, Thomas can sense the man staring fiercely at him, his mouth agape as if awaiting the right moment to break a lifelong silence. That stare always unnerves the boy, as though Joseph is the one person who can see into his soul and is silently saying, you're no priest, you're a heathen who longs to travel the world.

'He gives me the creeps,' Molly says. 'I'd hate to be alone with him.'

'Sure, he wouldn't have the wits to harm a fly,' Jack says again.

'Well, he gives me the creeps too,' Thomas replies, glad to take Molly's side. 'I often think he's spying on me when I'm out for a stroll. All of a slap I feel goose pimples down my back as if unseen eyes are watching me.'

'That would be your mother wondering why you're not working,' Molly teases him.

'Did I tell you about last week?' Thomas holds Molly as close as he dares in his arms. 'Jack and I were off lying in the sun, having a smoke by the train tracks on Booterstown Marsh. We were messing about with a knife and we said we'd become blood brothers. Jack had nicked his palm and I was about to do the same when Joseph came charging out from the reeds, grunting like a madman and scattering us with a hail of stones.'

'Maybe he was jealous,' Molly says, 'maybe he wants to be your blood brother. I mean, you and Jack both look an awful lot like him.'

She is teasing them both but Thomas can see that her eyes are really on Jack O'Driscoll, who shakes a fist at her in mock anger.

'You mind your tongue, or we may tie you up and dump you in his piggery,' Jack says. 'Joseph loves those pigs. If a pig is sick he'll sit up all night nursing it. The only thing he loves more than nursing them is slitting their throats when the time comes with his black-handled knife.' Jack runs a finger across his own throat and then steps back from the window in alarm. 'Look out, here's the missus striding up the avenue.'

There is a great scattering. Molly and Jack run for the back stairs that lead to the kitchen and Thomas snatches up the jazz record to hide it inside a leather-bound *Lives of the Saints* that he was meant to be reading. He hears his mother entering the hall, with her loud voice summoning his two brothers from the yard. He should go down to greet her; they are due to travel to Booterstown Church where he is serving as an altar boy at evening devotions. But he can still snatch ten minutes of freedom if he runs down the back stairs and slips out into the yard where the milk churns are stored.

The yard is quiet – not like at dawn, when he is always woken by the creak of donkeys and carts, the noise of voices and hobnailed boots. He hears his brother Pete calling him from inside the house, but he ignores the shout. Instead he sprints for freedom down the dusty length of Castledawson Avenue to where it joins the Rock Road. Here, tram tracks glisten in the evening light. If he could follow the tracks they would lead him into Dublin city, with its factories and teeming slums, its bird markets and street hawkers. If he could sneak away he would watch ships being loaded on the quays by bow-legged sailors who swap stories about foreign ports while pig-tailed Chinese cabin boys barely older than him spit out gobs of chewed tobacco like grown men.

The drone of an engine disturbs his thoughts as he stares down the Rock Road. He glances up, amazed to see an aeroplane swoop over the rooftops and playing fields of Blackrock College. The plane is directly overhead, the pilot in goggles tilting his wings to look down at the boy. Thomas begins to chase after the plane which swoops across the Rock Road and over Emmet Square towards the railway line and the coast. The magic of seeing a plane makes him forget about keeping his clothes clean to serve at benediction. If the pilot made a bumpy landing by the train tracks and offered to take Thomas on a short flight, where would he wish to go? With a shock, Thomas realises that he would wish to travel as far as the plane could take him; to all the foreign cities painted in gold leaf on Dr Thomson's radiogram; to places where nobody knew that his mother had declared he had a vocation; to places where he might see the world, not as a priest but as an adventurer.

Thomas stops running when he reaches the coastline

because the pilot has flown carelessly on, swinging out in the direction of Bull Island, which the boy can see across the bay. He is breathless, his trousers streaked with dust, his polished boots scuffed. Watching the plane become a speck, he is shocked by the vehemence of his wish. But he feels that the air is filled with voices if he could only hear them, the voices that might have whispered from Dr Thomson's radiogram, voices of distant cities calling out to him to find the courage to leave home.

There is a shout behind him and Jack O'Driscoll appears.

'That was a close shave with your ma,' Jack says with a grin. 'Your brother Pete is on the warpath.'

They walk back companionably towards Castledawson Avenue. But Thomas tries not to look over-familiar with the servant when he spies Pete waiting for him.

'Are you deaf, Thomas? Where were you dashing like a Zulu?'

Thomas glances back across the Rock Road, imagining the aeroplane wheeling over the sand dunes of Bull Island — that wilderness which his mother has promised he will be allowed to explore on some Sunday excursion by horse and trap, a mysterious heaven of oystercatchers and pale-bellied Brent geese to which he knows she is too practical to ever bother bringing him. He shrugs, sheepishly. 'Sure, where have I to go to except home?'

EIGHTEEN

Joey

November 2009

S hane stepped out from the car into the darkness of Bull Island. The wind was whipping sand up onto our faces and the clouds threatened rain, but he seemed to instinctively know which path to take. I didn't want to be left alone with that stolen car, so, awkwardly carrying the blue guitar, I tried to keep up with him, scrambling for my footing amidst the rabbit burrows and crumbling sandy tracks. We were in complete darkness, and after a few moments I lost sight of Shane and had no idea which direction to turn. Then Shane called my name, so softly that I barely heard it above the wind. I turned to see his outline standing on the crest of an enormous dune.

His back was turned as he calmly waited for me to join him. A shaft of moonlight broke through the clouds as I struggled up to the top. The view from there was breathtaking. All of Dublin Bay stretched before us: Howth to our left with its clusters of winking lights and then, amid its dark cliffs, a slow flash from the Baily lighthouse. But Shane's eyes were fixed across the Bay, staring towards the Booterstown marsh, then Williamstown, and Blackrock and Seapoint and Monkstown, towards that South Dublin coastline that I thought I knew well, but that I had never seen like this before, beautiful and out of reach.

'As a child I longed so much to come to Bull Island,' Shane said, 'but I could never persuade my mother to bring me. Sometimes you need to travel away from your home, Joey, before you can see it properly. When I want to see Blackrock in its entirety, this is where I come, because from here I can see every pinprick of light and imagine every life ever lived there and every life to come. Those are the lights your dad was rushing home to on the night he crashed, Joey. Your dad is one tiny part of Blackrock's story, but there are thousands of others with no one left to remember them. Four hundred shipwrecked souls were washed up on that shoreline in one night, poor conscripts who lost their lives when trapped in the holds of two transport ships battered against the rocks at Blackrock House. Their bodies lie in an unmarked pit in the tiny burial ground behind the Esso garage on the Merrion Road. Two summers ago I used to sit there because I had no one to talk to. Now sometimes I sit there just so I can talk to the dead.'

'Nobody can talk to the dead,' I said.

Shane turned to look closely at me in the moonlight. 'What makes you so sure?'

'Because it makes no sense.'

'Three girls spent hours getting ready to go out tonight, clowning around, laughing, bitching. One of them is now lying dead in a morgue. Does that make any sense? It could have been you or me, Joey.'

'Killed by your crazy driving.'

'No, killed by random chance, by the throw of a dice. Life is a gamble, Joey; death can come to claim us at any second. Driving across that wooden bridge, I could hear that special sound.'

'What sound?'

'The sound of how life is so finely balanced.' Shane stared out at the waves, his voice barely audible. 'I could hear our tyres bumping along the planks. I could hear the wing-beat of disturbed night birds, and rabbits bolting for cover and foxes raising their heads to listen. I knew what they were listening to because I heard that rustle too.'

'What rustle?'

'The rustle of the summoned dead.'

'You're cracked, Shane.'

'Am I? Don't tell me you didn't see them chasing in mid-air after the car?'

'Are you on drugs or what?'

'Surely you saw them, Joey, pressing against the car, beating on the glass. It was you they were there for – not trying to claim you, but to protect you. All those dead souls, frantic with worry for you. Only an extraordinary love could have summoned them. It was your father's love; I could see him among them.'

'Stop these lies now, Shane. I've had enough of your mind games.' I was so annoyed that I wanted to punch him, yet I was also weirdly intrigued.

'I have known extraordinary evil,' Shane replied, 'so I can recognise extraordinary love. I can't believe you didn't see him through the windscreen, his hands trying to slow the car, desperate to keep you safe. Our mad drive summoned him and he's still here, right behind you. I know because I have the power to see the dead. Don't bother looking around, because you obviously don't. But here's your chance to say the things you always wanted to say to him, Joey. This time he will really be able to hear.'

I wanted to call Shane a liar and a spoof, but out there in that dark wilderness, looking across at the lights of Blackrock, I didn't know what to believe any more. Or maybe the thought was just so tempting that I wanted to believe him. Because Shane's earlier manic energy was gone; he looked drained as he spoke again, 'I never meant to frighten you on the bridge, Joey, but my only way to summon him was to drive at that speed. I was bringing you to your gig, the gig you always dreamed of playing. Be honest: if you had a choice between playing the biggest venue in Europe or playing for your dad alone, you'd play for him here and now.'

Shane patted my shoulder and walked off through the darkness. I said nothing to him. I said nothing to anyone, because how could I when there was no one around? There was just the wind and the sea and the distant lights of my birthplace. But then – maybe because I needed to fill that silence – after a time, I spoke. I didn't know who I was addressing, just that I found myself saying things I had always wanted to say, words I could never utter to a living soul because they were too naked and confused to make any sense. But these were my true emotions: my expression of love for my lost dad, my sense that I could never fill his shoes or fill the aching void that seemed to still exist in my mum's life.

When I ran out of things to say, I picked up that stolen blue guitar and began to play, simply for myself, because who else was out there? I sang every song I had ever written and I sang them better than I had ever sung before. Finally, when I had no songs left, I just sat there in the dark. Then, from nowhere – though of course they had to come from inside my head – I heard words spoken. *That was sweet playing, Joey; you're going to be fine, son.* I didn't look up, but it felt like a weight had lifted off my shoulders.

Almost immediately, there was a sudden whoosh of flame. I looked around and realised that Shane had set the stolen car alight. Perhaps he did so to destroy any trace of our identities or maybe he meant it as a beacon to guide me back to him. But that burning car amid the sand dunes seemed like a funeral pyre for my father. I sensed that I would be all right, that we were saying goodbye to each other, letting one another move on. I felt eerily calm. Putting down the stolen guitar, I walked back towards Shane. When I reached the burning car we shook hands and raced through the dark to get off the island before anyone could catch us. As we crossed the wooden bridge, the tide was coming in, the water glistening so oddly in the moonlight that it felt like running through the landscape of a dream.

NINETEEN

Shane

August 2007

On the night they visited Thomas's house, Shane once again dreamed that water was about to engulf him. But this time, whispering voices populated his dream. When he woke, there was silence in the duplex on the site of the old convent on Sion Hill, but his heart beat so loudly he was certain it would wake his parents in the next bedroom. Shane longed to tell his dad about meeting the old man who had known his grandfather. Back in Sallynoggin, he had discussed everything with his dad on long evenings playing soccer together on the green opposite their old house. But Shane decided it was wiser to say nothing now, because his parents would be angry with him for breaking into that old dairy and would make him promise never to go back. Thomas was a disturbingly lonely figure, but during the next three days, Shane could not explain his overwhelming desire to return to that house.

Each morning, he met Geraldine as usual outside the library, but the easy familiarity between them was strained. They felt burdened by having sworn to keep Thomas's secret. They spent their time whispering and wondering what to do next. They hated to imagine anyone dying, but wanted to respect Thomas's wish to be allowed to do so alone. Yet Geraldine could not sleep with the thoughts of the pain Thomas might be in. Her gran noticed the change in her as she went into Geraldine's bedroom to turn off the light.

'You're very tense,' she said, 'is anything wrong?'

Curling up in the bed, Geraldine imagined Thomas lying alone on a damp mattress. She had seen little food in his house, and she worried that he might not have money to buy any.

'Do you mind if I take some food from the kitchen?' she asked. 'Just a few tins of soup and juices and that.'

Her gran stroked her hair. 'Fire away, if it's for a good cause. Is it for a sale-of-work?'

Avoiding the question, Geraldine asked her gran, 'Do I look like my mum?'

'Yes, especially when you smile. But at times you remind me of my own mum.'

'And your mother's maiden name was Fleming?'

'That's right.' She leaned over Geraldine. 'You look stressed. Is there anything you want to talk about?'

Geraldine wasn't used to keeping secrets from her gran. It was a horrible feeling.

'No,' she lied. 'I just want to go asleep, Gran.'

The next day, Geraldine raided the kitchen and filled an old pillowcase with food that she thought an elderly person might like. She asked Shane to meet her at the entrance to Castledawson Avenue after dinner. However, Shane's parents had such a row that it was dusk before he had patched up an uneasy truce between them and could safely slip away.

When they reached the old house, he suggested knocking at the front door, but Geraldine said that Thomas would not answer. So they climbed over the back wall and forced their way down the slope. Soon they were peering in through the basement window. It looked frighteningly dark in there, but Geraldine was determined to deliver the food. At least when she tried to sleep tonight, she would know that Thomas was not hungry.

They scrambled in through the window. Geraldine wanted to call out to Thomas, but felt unable to break the silence that seemed to weigh down on them as they left the kitchen and climbed the steps up into the hall. The room where they had encountered Thomas was empty. Everything was gone except for the bare mattress. Perhaps Thomas had checked himself into a hospital. Geraldine felt relieved to no longer be burdened with his secret. But Shane experienced an unfathomable disappointment, as if he had been summoned here by a sense of destiny he could not explain. They went back out to the hallway and Shane suggested that they explore upstairs. At the foot of the main stairs, he shone his torch up into the darkness. But it looked so frightening that neither of them seemed able to take the first step.

They hesitated, uncertain of what to do next. Then they were startled by a sudden smash of glass at their feet. Geraldine screamed and gripped Shane's hand. He switched on his torch. Neither of them knew what to expect.

TWENTY

Joey

November 2009

It was three a.m. when I got home from Bull Island, but I knew Mum would still be waiting up, reading a thriller from the library. I had to knock because I realised that I had left my key in my schoolbag in Shane's. Our house had not changed much since I was small. The rooms had been repainted several times, and last summer Mum had splashed out on a new sofa and carpet. But, essentially, the rooms seemed frozen in time since my childhood. This made our home feel like a haven where I would always be safe. Mum was more than just my mum; previously we had been too close to have secrets. But now, standing before her as she opened the front door, I felt robbed of the comforting sense of being safely home, because while I didn't want to lie to her, how could I tell her the truth about what I had been involved in tonight?

I knew Mum must have sensed this, because she said, 'I don't like what he's doing to you.'

'Who?'

'Your new friend. It's like he's trying to draw you away from me. Every time you come home after being with him I can see his influence subtly changing you.'

'Mum, you know you can't pick my friends.'

'Nor do I want to pick a fight with you. I always knew that one day you'd grow up and I wouldn't be part of your life in the same way again. Just don't hide things from me, Joey; it's the loneliest feeling in the world to have someone lie to you.'

'You don't have to be alone.' I felt a stab of betrayal for parroting Shane's words. 'It's not fair to blame your loneliness on me.'

'Is your friend saying I'm lonely? Is he even starting to colour how you see me? You can be alone without being lonely. The truth is, Joey, I was never willing to settle for second best after your dad died. We had a fiery relationship, but it was never dull. I always knew when he was up to something, though, and it's the same with you. When you walked in tonight and gave me that guilty smile, you were a dead ringer for him. The world is full of dangers at three a.m.'

'I wasn't in any danger,' I lied.

'There's more than one kind of danger.'

'I wasn't with a girl or anything.'

'I would know if you had been because I learned all the tell-tale signs.'

'Mum, let's not have this conversation.' I was scared that my perfect image of my father would be ruined. He had felt so close on Bull Island that I'd forgiven Shane for stealing the car, thinking Shane had orchestrated everything to bring me closer to my dad's spirit. Now, I had the uneasy sensation that Shane had arranged all this to drive a wedge between my mum and me.

She looked jaded as she headed from her bedroom. 'I want no secrets while you're under my roof. Like your dad, you have talent, but like him, you're also easily led. Take the guitar away from him and he was a bit of a lost soul. He always tried to find his way home but he could be easily led astray. It's time you knew this. Don't be led astray, Joey, especially by someone you can't trust.'

TWENTY-ONE

Shane

August 2007

When Shane shone his torch at Geraldine's feet in the hallway of the old house, he discovered the shards of an old-fashioned milk bottle shattered on the flagstones. They both wanted to run. The silence was broken by a guilty chuckle overhead.

'That was childish of me,' a voice said. 'But as a boy I always longed to toss a milk bottle over these banisters. My mother would have beaten me black and blue, but I suppose I can risk it now when there's no one left alive to tell me what to do.'

Shane's torch lit up Thomas's face leaning down to gaze at them. The beam was weaker than before, the batteries running low. Shane realised that he really didn't know whether this man was someone he could trust.

'You scared us,' Geraldine said indignantly. 'We could have been hurt.'

'That's true,' Thomas said. 'But I did tell you not to come back.'

'We brought food,' Geraldine explained. 'We're sorry if we're disturbing you, but we didn't know if you were hungry.'

Thomas turned his face away and when he looked back down, even though the torchlight was weak, Shane thought he saw tears in his eyes. 'You're not disturbing me,' he said softly. 'The greatest act of human kindness is to bring food to a hungry man.' Awkwardly, he wiped his eyes with his shirtsleeve and smiled. 'For that, you deserve a full tour of the house.' He saw them exchange a hesitant look. 'It won't take long, although it seems that my brothers never threw anything out.'

Thomas lit a candle and held it aloft as they slowly ascended the staircase to join him. Geraldine placed the food parcel at his feet and Thomas bent to examine it. 'Thank you again,' he said to Geraldine and then he looked at Shane. 'You're brave to come back, but your grandfather was also brave. Jack was a good friend to me. One part of me hoped I would see you again; another part of me prayed that you'd forget I exist.'

'We were worried about you,' Shane said.

'There's no need to worry. The doctors in America kindly gave me six to nine months to live.'

'How long ago was that?' Geraldine asked.

The old man smiled. 'Sometime between six and nine months ago. The tablets keep the worst of the pain at bay, but they are so strong they make me giddy. It means that when I'm not in pain I feel as lightheaded as a boy again.' He picked up a dusty milk bottle from the row assembled at his feet. 'Let's see who can strike the front door from here.' Leaning over the banisters he flung the bottle. It smashed on the flagstones, well short of its target. He offered Geraldine a bottle.

'You can't throw bottles inside a house,' Geraldine protested.

'Why not?'

'You just can't. It's … ' Geraldine searched for the word her gran would use, '… irresponsible.'

'True,' Thomas agreed. 'But the time to be responsible is when one is a lot older than you are now and a lot younger than me. Finally, this is my house, where no tyrant of a mother can tell me what to do.'

'I'll throw one so,' Shane volunteered. 'I bet you I can hit the door too.'

'I'll expect nothing less.' Thomas handed him the bottle. 'Seeing as it was your grandfather who thought up this game. I just needed to wait three-quarters of a century to play it. Molly and Jack used to laugh about what my mother would do if we actually tried this. Go ahead, fill Jack's shoes.'

Thomas made it sound like a test. Shane hurled a milk bottle that smashed inches short of the front door. He enjoyed the sensation and the thought that somehow his grandfather's boyhood ghost might be watching. 'Have a go,' he urged Geraldine, but she was still reluctant until Thomas placed a dusty bottle in her hands.

'Last winter I was in a New Jersey asylum,' he said. 'Not because I was mad, but you learn to fake madness when your bones are too old to spend another winter sleeping on the streets. An attorney tracked me down to say that I had inherited this property. The site is worth millions as development land. It's funny – all my life I had time and no money. Now when I finally have money, I'm running out of time. Soon this will be no one's home, Geraldine, so be irresponsible; break anything you like because some developer will dump all my brothers' hoarded possessions into a skip and nobody will remember the lives lived here.'

Geraldine flung the bottle over the banisters and gave a guilty giggle when it smashed on the flagstones. She thought of how, in time, everything – even her treasure trove box of mementos – would eventually wind up in a skip; of how everything is forgotten when there is no one left to remember. But she didn't dwell on such dark thoughts because the throwing contest developed into a frantic free-for-all. It was finally Shane who struck the front door. He bowed as Geraldine applauded and Thomas presented him with a chocolate bar from the food they had brought.

'My apologies for not having a bigger prize; you see, I will only become rich after I sell this house. But I have refused the solicitors permission to put it up for sale until they are certain I am dead.'

'How will they know?' Geraldine asked shyly.

'Once a week, I phone them when I slip out to buy food and painkillers. They have instructions to break down the front door if they receive no phone call for three weeks. They will find me dead here with directions for my funeral. They will also find my will hidden away. I haven't finalised it yet, because I am not sure who to leave my wealth to. Maybe I should leave it to one of you. Why do I feel that you have a secret wish to be rich, Shane?'

'I didn't come here for money,' Shane said, embarrassed. 'We came to bring you food.'

'That means a lot to me,' the old man said, 'because I have known true hunger. When the taste of hunger gets inside you, you never lose it. I remember once eating berries on the side of the Dublin mountains at dawn when I was sent to collect someone. It was the first thing I had eaten in days. Since then, I have often been hungry for food, hungry for peace of mind, hungry most of all for human company. All my life, I've been cursed with a restless soul. So many cities, so many labouring jobs, so many trains and open roads, so many beaches to comb at dawn for anything washed up that I could salvage or save. You can cope with an empty stomach, but the most terrible hunger of all is to go through life starved of human companionship.'

Thomas closed his eyes and Shane could only guess at what loneliness he was remembering. The candle flickered and the boy was afraid that it was about to go out, but when Thomas opened his eyes the flame grew still.

'My gran will be worried about me,' Geraldine said. 'We have to go.'

Thomas nodded. 'That's wise,' he murmured. But as the teenagers made to leave, he slumped forward. Putting both hands to his face, he rocked back and forth.

'Are you in pain?' Geraldine asked, concerned.

Thomas lowered his hands to stare at the girl. His eyes looked different than they did a moment before. Shane couldn't decide if they were wistful or cunning as they turned their gaze towards him. 'I prayed you wouldn't come back, young O'Driscoll, but a more selfish part of me hoped you would. I haven't much strength left and there's one task I can't do on my own.'

'What task?' Shane asked.

'Old houses are like old people: full of secrets. This house was not originally a dairy.'

'What was it?'

'A prosperous merchant named Michael Byrne built it.' Thomas slowly rose to his feet. 'The reason why he built it on this exact spot has been covered up for over a century. Byrne was a man who made enemies. The nobility regarded him as an upstart because he started life with nothing. He was only a young servant boy when he discovered the corpse of his former master, the notorious rake, Henry Dawson, who once owned Castledawson House.'

'How did he make his fortune?' Shane asked.

'Some people called it peasant cunning; others said that he had the devil's own luck. He was a gambler; he had a set of dice shaped out of human bone with which he could never lose. By the time he died, he owned a dozen properties around Blackrock, though he could never buy the one he craved – Castledawson House. The new owners, who had bought it after Henry Dawson died, refused to sell it to him. Every few years, Michael Byrne would disappear on terrible drinking binges and turn up at the gates of Castledawson House, shouting "I want it back." '

'You said he had only been Henry Dawson's servant there,' Geraldine said.

'When he could not get Castledawson House, he built this new house for himself directly opposite the gates of the estate where he used to work. He never forgot the hunger of being a serving boy. He gave freely to the poor. In times of cholera he walked fearlessly among the dying, administering alms and what comfort he could. They say that, for all his vices, there was a touch of the saint in him. But the luck of every gambler runs out.' Thomas McCormack beckoned for them to follow. 'It was a sensation when Michael Byrne was found in the cellar of this house with his own throat cut. Now, let me show you a secret known to nobody else alive.'

TWENTY-TWO

Joey

November 2009

When I woke the next morning, I could scarcely believe that the previous night's events had occurred. I had intended merely to study in Shane's house. Instead, I had watched a girl die, taken part in a car theft and revealed my most intimate feelings to what was either a ghostly presence or simply the empty night air. In the morning light, I knew that Shane was either a fantasist or a spoof, but his description of hordes of anxious ghosts pressing against our speeding car kept haunting my mind.

Mum said little over breakfast. The relaxed intimacy we once took for granted seemed to have disappeared. When she turned up Temple Hill to drop me off outside the school on her way to work, I was relieved to escape from the silence of the car, from her unspoken accusation that I was allowing myself to be groomed for something. I hoped that Shane would remember my schoolbag, yet I also dreaded meeting him. We all do crazy things at times, but last night Shane had possessed such a manic determination to bring me to Bull Island that he could have killed someone in the process. I didn't want him bragging about our exploits in class, especially as Mum had gone to huge trouble to enrol me here and the last thing she deserved was more hassle.

When I entered the classroom before our history exam, Shane was there before me, my schoolbag left on my desk. I thought he was ignoring me, but then I realised that he was jotting down history notes. He walked towards me.

'Here are those dates you were having trouble with. Memorise a few of them and Bongo Drums will think you're a genius.'

He handed me a neatly written list. There was no wild-ness visible on his features now, just a parental concern. None of our classmates would believe the things he had done a few hours before, and I realised that Shane would never mention them to anyone. Last night's anarchy was filed away in a sealed compartment. How many other such compartments existed in Shane's life? I thought of his de-scription of himself on the quays: a beachcomber comb-ing for souls – how weird was that? It was an image of isolation, a solitary figure on the seashore scanning the horizon for jetsam and flotsam; scavenging the bits and pieces washed up from other people's lives.

Then Bongo Drums arrived and announced that the exam would start in two minutes. I forgot about every-thing except memorising Shane's list of dates before the test began.

Amazingly, almost every date on the list came up in some question, as if Shane had managed to second-guess

Bongo Drums' mind. I had never previously filled so many pages in an exam because everything we'd studied in Shane's room remained fresh in my mind. Midway through the test, Geraldine glanced back at me and smiled. For a moment, all thoughts of history vanished. Her hair looked beautiful in the sunlight, her neck so white. She caught me staring back and silently tut-tutted, urging me to focus on the exam questions. Then she blushed slightly and looked away and I knew that I loved her.

At the bell there was a relieved clamour of voices. I had forgotten to bring in a drink, so at break-time I got permission to visit the shops down the road. I bought a can of Coke and was drinking it on my way back to school when I experienced the overwhelming sensation of being watched. I turned to find that an old man was following me. He glared at me fiercely, hobbling forward on a walking stick until we were face-to-face. He wore an old hat and a long black overcoat. His eyes were bloodshot.

'Tell your friend I want it back,' he hissed.

'I beg your pardon?'

'You heard. Tell him I'll not be tricked out of what is rightfully mine any longer.'

Cars were speeding along the road, other students hurrying past to beat the bell, but I had never felt more alone than in those few seconds. What freaked me out most was that his eyes seemed oddly familiar, like eyes that I saw every day if I could only just place them. This old man's voice never rose above a whisper, but there was a vehemence within him that was frightening. The bell had rung. I wanted to walk back through the school gates and join my fellow students strolling into class, but I felt paralysed by the piercing gaze of those eyes that seemed younger than his body.

'Tell him I want it back, Joey,' he hissed.

'How do you know my name?'

'You may be a naïve fool, but you're a good boy. Don't be used by him. Help me, Joey; be my friend.'

The yard had emptied. At any moment Bongo Drums would come out to check the gates.

'I don't know what you're talking about.' I said. 'I have to go back to school.'

He looked wistfully in through the gates. 'Why did you let him lead you so astray last night?'

'What do you know about last night?'

'What do you know about him? It's typical of him to groom a shy kid who's been bullied. That's why your mother got you into this school, wasn't it?'

'Leave my mother out of this!'

'I know where you live, Joey. I know more about you than you could ever believe.'

'Are you related to Shane?'

He gave a bitter laugh. 'Let's just say we are linked through bad blood.'

'I don't know what you want.' I felt perturbed. I hated conversations where people expected you to know what they were talking about and made you feel like a fool for asking.

'I want you to ask yourself, what does he really want

from you? Why does he think he can have you as a friend when I'm the only friend he can have?' The old man glanced towards Bongo Drums who appeared at the gate. 'Tell him that one of us should not still be here. Tell him I want it back.'

TWENTY-THREE

Shane

August, 2007

Thomas led Shane and Geraldine downstairs, past the smashed milk bottles in the hallway. The only light came from the candle he held aloft and from the ever-weakening beam of Shane's torch. Entering the kitchen, Thomas opened the small door that they had noticed on the first night, the one which led into a narrow sloping corridor. He glanced back to ensure they were following. Geraldine wished that she had told her gran where she was going; she wished that she had told her gran everything. She tried to send her a text, but could get no signal in this basement. She followed Shane because she was scared of being left alone. Shane was fascinated by the idea that this house possessed a secret, but he was scared too. His fear arose from the odd sensation that somehow he had allowed himself to be groomed for this moment; that he had been in this cellar before if he could only remember.

At the end of the passageway, Thomas stooped his head to enter a bare storeroom. He waited for them to join him. The faint beam on Shane's torch gave out, so that the only light came from Thomas's candle and from the glow of Shane and Geraldine's mobile phones. The way the walls curved inwards made the cellar feel even smaller. If they got trapped here, nobody would ever find them. Thomas set down the candle on a flagstone.

'You think there's nothing to see, don't you?'

'I would like us to go back up to the kitchen,' Geraldine said, with nervous defiance.

Thomas sank to his knees. 'As a child I entered this cellar a hundred times, never thinking that it contained a secret either.' He looked up. 'After tonight you must promise never to return here. My time has come to die; indeed, my time is long overdue. I have outlived all the others. But before I die, there is something I wish to see one last time. Feel carefully along the rim of this main flagstone. It has a tiny cleft you can grip.'

Geraldine knelt and at first could feel nothing but then her fingers found the concealed edge. Soon all three of them had managed to gain a grip on the heavy stone and hoist it so that one side was resting on the adjoining flagstone. Everyone took a deep breath.

'We can drag it the rest of the way,' Thomas said. When they hauled the flagstone away from the chasm that opened up in the floor, the cellar felt even colder. Thomas raised the candle and its flame flickered, leaving Geraldine afraid that it would blow out. Then the flame steadied and, as she looked down into the black space where the stone had been, she saw a second candle flame appear and, alongside it, black hair and her own scared eyes staring back up at her. Realising that she was staring down into water so still that it acted as a mirror, Geraldine shivered and moved back.

'I'm scared of water,' she whispered. 'My mother drowned.'

'Yes, I know,' Thomas replied quietly.

'How could you know that?' Geraldine asked, startled.

Thomas looked at her as if caught out. 'You told me on the first night we met,' he said quietly.

'I never did. I never talk about her.'

'She drowned out in the bay, a sudden cramp in her leg like the grip of a claw reaching up from hell,' Thomas replied, almost absent-mindedly now, staring into the well as if hypnotised. 'Michael Byrne built his house on top of this well so that his water supply could not be poisoned by his enemies. My two brothers lived here all their lives, yet they never knew this well existed.'

'Who told you, so?' Shane shivered as he realised why this place felt familiar. It was the cellar he had been dreaming about for months. This was the well his father had dreamed about, seeping up through the floorboards of their old house.

'I was told by a man who couldn't talk.' Thomas gave a softly bitter laugh. 'A man related to me through bad blood.'

'How deep is it?' Shane was unable to stop himself from leaning over the water, fascinated by his own reflection.

'It looks shallow, merely a foot or two deep, but it is deceptive. Should you fall, it is deep enough to drown in, deep enough to disappear for ever.'

Geraldine tried to pull Shane back, but something caught his eye.

'I see a small set of dice down there,' Shane said. 'They are the strangest-looking things. I think I can reach them.' His outstretched hand had almost disturbed the water when Thomas gripped it fiercely.

'Disturb nothing,' the old man hissed savagely.

'Let go of my wrist,' Shane snapped, 'I just wanted to see what they were made of.'

'They look like bones,' Geraldine said in fascinated horror.

Thomas released his grip on Shane's wrist. He seemed lost in a world of his own. 'They're relics,' Thomas said, 'the bones of a saint.'

'Human bone!' Geraldine gasped.

'Anyone who gambles with those dice will always get their wish,' Thomas went on. 'I rolled the dice and made two wishes here at your age: a wish for myself and a wish for the man who became my blood brother.' From his coat pocket, Thomas produced a small, black-handled knife. 'He nicked our two wrists with this blade and held them together until our blood merged.'

Shane edged away from the water, acutely aware of the knife glistening in the weak candlelight.

'What happened after you made your wish?' he asked.

'Isn't that obvious?' Thomas raised the knife and flicked it with all his strength into the well. The sudden splash was amplified by the low walls, making Geraldine and Shane jump. 'I got my deepest wish – which is the greatest tragedy that can happen to anyone.'

TWENTY-FOUR

Joey

November 2009

Bongo Drums leaned against the school gate to watch the old man shuffle off.

'So, who's your new friend, Joey?' he asked wryly.

'I never saw him before, sir. I couldn't get away from him.'

'What class should you be in?'

'Double science.'

'Tell Shakes … Mr Sweeney … that I delayed you, waffling on about my days in rock bands. He complains that I bore the backside off him doing the same thing.'

'Were you really a drummer, sir?'

'Not a great one, but drummers don't have to be.' Bongo Drums chuckled with self-mockery. 'A drummer just needs to keep time and wink at the girls near the stage. There's no money in music, though there's always talk of big money just around the corner. A time comes when you need to settle down, but I used to love knocking out a living on the road.'

Gazing around the empty yard with bored eyes, Bongo Drums began to drone on about his glory days, name-checking bands that meant nothing to me. I was so fazed by the encounter with the old man that I wasn't even listening properly until I heard my father's name mentioned.

'Sorry, sir, what did you just say?'

'I said I even played with your dad for a spell.'

'I never knew you knew him.'

'I can't say I really did. Dessie Kilmichael was a maverick – difficult to play with, always changing the playlist, adding in guitar solos he made up on the spot. With a normal singer you played a normal set, you knew where you stood, but whenever I gigged with your father I had to be a mind-reader.'

'Was my dad any good?'

'It depends on how you define "good". He wasn't consistent because he was chasing after a sound nobody else heard. Some nights he was a genius, setting the place alight. Other nights he'd leave the audience behind and all we got from the punters was the rubber handclap. But I've never heard anyone like him before or since. Dessie once told me that he wanted to write one great song that would make him immortal. It was only last year when I found some demo tapes we'd made that I realised how unique he was.'

'You have tapes of him playing?'

'Only rough cuts. Still, they have his magic,' Bongo said. 'Dessie was a perfectionist, always buying more studio time to work on his famous album that never came out. His problem was that every time he did a take he did it differently.' Bongo Drums became aware of something in my gaze. 'But … I mean, you've heard his demos?'

'No. I've never heard him sing.'

'Come off it. The night I heard you play at that retreat in Wicklow, I made the connection between your names. No disrespect, but the way you bend certain chords is a direct rip-off of his style.'

'My mum destroyed all of his tapes.'

Bongo Drums laughed incredulously, then realised that I was serious. 'Why?'

'She just did.'

Bongo nodded soberly. 'I don't know if I could find those tapes again with so much junk in my attic. Still, if you wanted me to, I'd take a look.'

I had often fantasised about finding a recording of Dad, but now, confronted with the chance to hear his voice I didn't know if I could face the prospect of having my illusions shattered. What if he was not a genius? What if, despite all the myths, his songs were second-rate?

'I'd like to ask my mum first.'

'Yeah, you do that.' The teacher was scrutinising my face, searching for signs of my dead father's features. I wanted to tell him to stop, yet I wanted him to find my father rekindled within me. It was an uncomfortable sensation.

TWENTY-FIVE

Thomas

August 2007

Thomas McCormack remained alone in the cellar for a long time after Shane and Geraldine left, although he needed to go upstairs for more morphine before the pain became too intense to do anything except scream. His body required constant medication and proper medical care, but despite his intense loneliness and the pain, he knew that every new person he came into contact with was another potential victim whom the voices could use.

He knew this because he had been a victim once too, scared by a knife in this cellar. It had been wrong to produce the black-handled knife in front of Shane and Geraldine, but a part of him had hoped to frighten the boy away. More selfish voices inside him, though, were trying to tempt the boy back. The incessant babble of the Blackrock dead: the battle between those souls who longed to end this limbo and the others who wanted to find another victim whose body they could hijack to cling on to immortality for another lifetime.

It was hard to hear his own conscience amid all these whispering voices. Doctors in asylums had called it schizophrenia, bipolar split personality disorder. Thomas called it the curse of immortality, the loneliness of being neither truly alive nor fully dead.

He had left Blackrock to thwart those voices, to hide himself away in the foreign cities that he had longed to see as a boy. But the voices in his head were like a swarm of bees who found a crack in every door he ever closed over, because you cannot thwart an impulse that is stronger than life itself. For years, the voices had been plotting their survival, creeping into other people's dreams. They had gnawed away at Shane's father's peace of mind, convincing him that he needed to uproot his family. They had manifested themselves into the shape of a cramp that drowned a strong swimmer at sea and left her young daughter vulnerable.

Those voices would do anything to survive. They had tempted him into revealing this well to Shane and Geraldine. He begged God that the boy would not be tempted to return, but God had little to do with this cellar. Out in the overgrown garden, a black cat was watching, a cat who once prowled the ruins of the Hellfire Club. If Shane came back, Thomas swore that he would not let him in, that he would not aid the voices who had tricked him down into this cellar seventy years ago. Closing his eyes and trying to ignore the pain, Thomas McCormack relived the consequences of that childhood morning again.

TWENTY-SIX

Thomas

August 1932

Fourteen-year-old Thomas McCormack wakes to the familiar hubbub of carts and milk churns in the yard. He gets up at once because any sign of laziness irks his mother, who believes that no honest soul should be idle after sunrise. School restarts in two weeks' time, but for now there is still the prospect of freedom. Jack O'Driscoll will soon start his milk deliveries to houses on Carysfort Avenue and Newtownpark Avenue. As Thomas walks down to the kitchen he hatches a plan to join him. If the two friends work as a team, they will be able to find time to sneak away to smoke Woodbines and chase after imaginary Zulus through the fields behind Newtownpark House.

This plan depends on his mother letting him slip off to pursue his religious studies. Although she makes his brothers slave during every hour of daylight, she feels it her duty to allow Thomas to immerse himself in religious books that she gets on loan for him from the Holy Ghost fathers in Castledawson House in Blackrock College. Thomas dutifully tries to read them but you can only keep your mind on God for so long when there is the Booterstown shoreline to explore with Molly and Jack, if they can snatch any idle moments, or when he can walk to Dún Laoghaire pier to watch the boats departing across Dublin Bay and wonder about what type of journeys the passengers are embarking on.

In the kitchen, Molly serves him breakfast and asks for his help in rinsing out all the empty milk bottles later on.

'I do be exhausted by the time the Missus asks me,' she says, 'and – no disrespect to your mother – but by the way she fusses, you'd swear they were priceless antiques.'

'If Mammy goes out we can sit up on the landing and see who can hit the front door with a milk bottle first,' he jokes.

Molly laughs. 'Only ever try that if I'm safely on a boat to England. Even then I wouldn't feel safe in case she'd unleashed a tidal wave to capsize us.'

Thomas loves to make Molly laugh, but he knows that she is in love with Jack O'Driscoll. He saw it in the way she danced with Jack to the jazz record last week. He tries to think of something else that would make Molly smile, but she leaves the kitchen to finish her other chores. Quickly, he finishes breakfast and then crosses the bustling yard in search of his mother. Loose straw blows about. There is a stench of cow dung and he has to shoo away a stray black cat who has wandered in. He pauses to stroke the old donkey harnessed to the nuns' cart, surprised that their servant, Joseph, hasn't already departed with the milk churns for the convent. The mute hunchback is nowhere to be seen, but then he emerges from an outhouse and limps towards the kitchen door. Glancing into the empty kitchen, Joseph turns to give a gap-toothed smile and urgently beckons Thomas towards him with his crippled hand.

Thomas is wary of Joseph. The old man is regarded as a harmless idiot, so docile that he grins even if young lads throw sods at him as he drives around the side-streets of Monkstown looking for slops for his pigs. But on several occasions Thomas has seen the donkey cart halted by the shore at Blackrock House and Joseph staring fixatedly out to sea for hours, grunting furiously as if caught up in some imaginary conversation inside his head.

Joseph now strides into the kitchen, even though he is not allowed near the house. Thomas doesn't want Molly to find herself alone with him if she returns. He follows Joseph into the kitchen and orders the man out. Normally Joseph is timid, but this morning there is something different about him. Instead of leaving, he grips Thomas's jacket with a brute strength. Joseph's eyes look bloodshot and unnaturally large. His skin is blotched and his breath stinks. The nuns boast about him being the neatest slaughterer of pigs in the district. Pigs trust him. They willingly enter the pen, thinking he is going to give them a special treat. And he has a tender way of gazing into their eyes before cutting their throats with the black-handled knife he always keeps wrapped in a rag inside his coat. Joseph can barely recognise the letters of the alphabet, but nobody knows more about gaining the trust of animals. Suddenly, Thomas knows how those pigs must feel, because there is

something hypnotic in the man's gaze as he makes sooth-
ing grunts as if to reassure him.

Thomas finds himself pushed down a passageway towards the tiny cellar. He feels powerless and tries to pray.
If Joseph cuts his throat the man will hang for it in Moun-
tjoy Jail. Thomas can imagine him refusing to let the hang-
man place a black sack over his head, fixing him with a
stupefied gaze as the trapdoor opens.

They enter the tiny cellar, which acts as a store for broken machinery. This is the last place where anyone would
look for him. As Joseph unwraps his black-handled knife
Thomas tries to scream but no sound comes. The man
kneels and beckons the boy to do likewise. His manic grin
is hypnotic. Thomas sinks down, expecting to feel a stab
when Joseph raises the knife. Instead the blade plunges
downwards, dislodging some cement from around the
largest flagstone.

The man works frantically, occasionally glancing up to
grin at the boy. What is underneath the flagstone, Thomas
wonders – maybe a deeper cellar, unknown to anyone?
Has Joseph killed other children and hidden them in this
black hole? The prospect that his body might never be
found is more chilling than death itself. Joseph wedges his
fingers under the heavy flagstone and, grunting, manages
to drag it to one side. Thomas leans forward to stare into
the abyss. He gasps when he sees his own reflection staring back up at him.

He is looking down into a well that looks no more than
two or three feet deep. But Thomas senses that if he were

to place his weight on the loose stones at the bottom they would give way beneath him, causing him to keep falling downwards. Joseph is mumbling, a strangulated babble, as he points towards two tiny dice lying on the loose stones. The man no longer seems threatening as he guides Thomas's hand towards the ice-cold water. The boy wonders who else knows about this well. It is impossible to guess at the secrets that Joseph must know. Even the nuns have no idea how old he is. Nobody in Blackrock could remember a time when he wasn't around and everyone talks openly in front of him because they know that he can repeat nothing.

Thomas reaches down and manages to retrieve the dice with his fingertips. They are made of something peculiar that he cannot place. There is a novelty in holding dice because his mother refuses to allow gambling or card games in the house. Joseph is gesturing for him to throw them back into the water. Instead Thomas tosses them onto the flagstones and, to his delight, rolls a double six. He tosses them a second time and his luck is still in, because once again he rolls the same number. 'I should win something,' he says half-jokingly to Joseph. 'What do I win?'

The mute grunts again but this time the boy instinctively senses what he is trying to express.

'Are you saying I win the right to make a wish?'

The grunting stops. Thomas has never known any expression to be so serious. Joseph nods towards the water. The boy is tempted to laugh because the notion is ridiculous, but Joseph looks so earnest that Thomas decides to keep him happy. He leans forward. As he stares down he can see both their reflections. But Joseph's reflection looks different in the water, as if all the deformities of birth have been smoothed away. Thomas gazes deeper into the well, overcome by the idea that unseen faces are lurking there. The further the bricks in the wall of the well sink down, the less they resemble bricks. Instead, they shimmer like the rough outline of distant cities. This is my wish, Thomas thinks. I wish to travel the world. He is about to toss the dice into the water when Joseph grips his fingers, grunting frantically.

'What is it?' Thomas asks. 'Do you want to hear my wish? I don't want to be a priest, ordered to go only where my bishop commands. I wish to be free to travel through all the foreign cities on this earth.'

Shocked by the vehemence of his own desire, Thomas tosses the dice into the well and watches them descend slowly through the water. They settle on the stones in two perfect sixes. With a shudder of horror he realises what they are made out of: bone. Something makes him think it's human bone.

'What would you wish for, Joseph?' he asks.

Joseph rocks back and forth, too tongue-tied to speak. Then his finger frantically stabs at the small pile of cement dirt. Thomas realises that he is shaping a crude outline of the numeral 2.

'2?' Thomas asks.

Joseph nods fiercely, scattering the dirt again to draw

another shape. It looks like a crooked squiggle until Thomas makes out the shape of the letter B.

'B?' he asks. '2B?'

Froth coats Joseph's lips, but his eyes are ecstatic. Then they grow weary as he smoothes out the dirt. He appears confused. To be what: to be able to speak, to ride in a motorcar, to sleep in a bed with clean sheets? Thomas feels that he will never know Joseph's wish because the man slumps down, defeated. This is his chance to flee, but he has only taken one step towards the door when Joseph's left hand grips his jacket. Thomas looks down to see Joseph's right hand drawing the shape of a bowl in the dust. Then Thomas realises it is the letter U.

'2 B U?' Thomas asks. He feels uneasy. 'You want to be me?'

Joseph nods and drags the boy down beside him. Producing the black-handled knife, he nicks Thomas's palm and then slices open his own flesh. Disgusted, Thomas tries to break free but Joseph grips his hand so tight that blood from the two wounds mingles as he plunges their hands towards the dice in the well. Thomas closes his eyes, shocked at how the cold water stings the wound and then stunned because the wound seems to suddenly heal.

He feels swamped by so many new emotions that he needs to keep his eyes closed while he tries to understand the sudden onslaught of strange memories – memories he could not possibly possess. Suddenly he knows what it feels like to toast the devil with drunken rakes in the mountains; to kneel among cholera victims, holding water to their dying lips; to gamble with crooked dice as an up-start; to be starved and eat berries on a mountainside; to be trapped inside the hold of a transport ship in a storm at sea. He can recall so many strange things that his brain feels like it has been invaded by an incessant swarm of voices.

He wants to ask Joseph what has happened, but of course Joseph cannot speak. However, now when Thomas tries to form words, he finds that it is he who cannot speak. Only grunts emerge. He hears Joseph drag the flag-stone back into place, but he is still too afraid to open his eyes, unsure of what face will greet him. Then he is hauled to his feet and shoved back into the passageway. It is only when he bumps into the wall that he is forced to finally open his eyes and confront his own face which is staring back at him.

In the kitchen Molly looks up as two figures emerge from the passageway. 'What is Joseph doing in the house?' she asks. 'The missus will be furious.' Then she stops and stares at Thomas. 'Are you all right?'

His eyes look different to her, like an old man's eyes, like eyes that have just seen a procession of ghosts.

TWENTY-SEVEN

Joey

November 2009

I left Bongo Drums in the yard and entered the science lab. Shakes was so involved in an experiment that he barely looked up. The class was engrossed, like they always were when the science teacher started messing with test tubes and heaters. It seemed impossible that any hand with such a tremor could safely transfer a bubbling concoction between test tubes. Tales of Shakes's eyebrows being burned off in explosions in previous experiments were too legendary to be true. But silence always reigned in the lab when he uttered the words, 'this is highly dangerous' and set to work with shaking fingers. Shane sat at the back of the class. Other students squeezed up to make space, acknowledging my rightful place beside him.

'Shakes is a showman,' Shane observed quietly. 'That tremor is purely to get our attention.'

'It's a medical condition,' I said.

'You only see tremors like that in alcoholics seeking a cure.'

'How would you know?'

Shane sounded miles away. 'I've seen enough alcoholics in taverns and back alleys,' he muttered, distractedly.

'They say my own father was an incurable drunk. Drink killed him.'

'Alcohol didn't kill your father,' I said sharply. 'He burned to death.'

Shakes looked up, annoyed by our voices.

'Have you gentlemen a comment you wish to share with us?'

'I was remarking that your perseverance in the face of physical disability is an inspiration to us all, sir.'

There was no trace of sarcasm in Shane's voice as he spoke. His tone was sanctimonious and inscrutable: a voice to hide behind. The golden rule in science was never to mention Shakes's tremor. But Shane's mask of absolute sincerity left the teacher with no option but to resume the experiment.

'You're pushing your luck,' I whispered.

Shane shrugged. 'At least I showed up for his class. What kept you this late?'

'I met a crazy old man.'

'That only rules out the female teachers.'

'He was no teacher. The one thing keeping him alive was anger and all his anger was directed at you.'

'Me?' Shane glanced up with guarded eyes. 'Why me?'

'He claims you have something belonging to him. Whatever it is, he wants it back.'

Shane made no reply, but stared up at Shakes who had concluded the experiment. I saw that Shane was rattled. He raised a hand to ask Shakes a complex question. The teacher had been annoyed, but now he was flattered by

Shane, expressing delight that at least one person in class had fully grasped the principles. But I knew that Shane had no interest in the experiment. He was buying himself time before having to reply to me.

Eventually the bell went for lunch and I followed Shane through the bustling corridor. We went out into the yard and sat on the steps, away from most people.

'Talk to me, Shane,' I said. 'That old guy scared the wits out of me.'

'What does he want back?'

'He didn't say. He said you were related through bad blood.'

Shane gave a quiet, bitter laugh. 'Yeah, we're twins.'

'It's not funny, Shane. Who the hell is he?'

Shane took out a sandwich. 'His name is Thomas McCormack. He's a paranoid schizophrenic who was a tramp in America before he inherited a run-down house on Castledawson Avenue. Geraldine and I made the mistake of breaking in there one night. Not to rob him or anything. We thought the gaff was deserted. He fed us a sob story about being at death's door. I only called to see him two other times, but he made my life hell in the months afterwards, turning up at my house and shouting that I'd stolen something.'

'Stolen what?'

'I have no idea. I wouldn't mind but there was nothing worth stealing in his gaff. Never befriend a loner, Joey, because they grow obsessed with you. They have no one else to blame, so they blame you for everything. I'm not saying he caused the fire in which my folks died. But he got my mum so paranoid that she couldn't sleep. Anyone can forget to switch off a chip pan, but maybe the fire wouldn't have happened if she wasn't chewing tranquillisers to cope with him always turning up and wrecking her head with lies.'

Geraldine was sitting nearby with two girls. I glanced over, but she always refused to look in my direction when I was with Shane.

'So why is he hassling me?' I asked.

'He has this notion that only he can be my true friend. He hates when I get close to anyone else. I have a laugh here with folk at school but I never make close friends because I know that old man will try to poison them against me.'

'Have you not gone to the police?'

Shane snorted. 'My dad used to call the cops when he'd turn up. They even locked Thomas up in John of God's until he fooled them into thinking he was sane again so he could get back to his pigsty of a house. I hoped that when I returned from England he would be dead, but he has been stalking me since my return.'

'What do I do about him?'

'Ignore him, Joey. Trust me; that man is due a blind date with death soon. He has no right to still be alive.'

The bell went for the end of lunch break. Lads were kicking a tennis ball. It flew in our direction. Shane caught it. 'Next goal the winner,' he shouted, lunging into them. Dribbling past two players, he aimed a shot at the bin that the lads were using as a makeshift goal. Some lads claimed the goal didn't count; others tipped off quickly to get an equaliser before a teacher broke up the game. Shane chased after the ball, looking carefree – utterly different from the person I had been talking to a moment before.

Trust me, Shane had said. I didn't know which Shane to trust anymore because there seemed to be so many of them. Geraldine passed by. I wanted to ask her advice, but mentioning Shane would only drive her further away, when what I most wanted was to get to know her. Because I knew by how she occupied my every waking thought and by how her presence made any classroom or corridor special, that I was in love with her.

Bongo Drums appeared and broke up the match, un-able to resist kicking the tennis ball himself. The lads teased him as they walked back to class. As he grinned good-naturedly I tried to imagine him playing drums in my father's band. Shane drifted beside me as I walked indoors. His face was serious, the mask of good humour gone.

'If you'd like us to stop hanging out together that's cool.'

'No,' I replied, because I wasn't sure what else to say. I didn't have the words to express my increasing sense of unease. 'I mean, we're mates.'

He smiled. 'You and I are closer than mates, Joey. One of these days we'll nick our palms with a knife and become blood brothers.'

TWENTY-EIGHT

Shane

August 2007

Geraldine and Shane spent the day after their second visit to Thomas's house trying to avoid one another. They felt burdened by responsibility because nobody else knew about the dying man. Geraldine was tormented by worries about how long it would take Thomas to die from his cancer, whether his pain would become utterly unbearable without medical help and whether they would get into trouble after he was found dead in that empty house.

Shane found it easier to keep secrets because his parents kept so many secrets from him. The secret of how much money they owed. The secret lottery scratch cards Shane kept finding in the bin. The secret figures that Shane's father crossed out on the back of newspapers. Last night, after his return from Thomas's house, his parents had argued with ferocious intensity, as if an insatiable rage was tearing his family apart. The row continued until dawn, with Shane lying awake, fantasising about finding any way, no matter how outlandish, to get the money to buy some peace in this new home that he hated.

It was eight o'clock in the evening when Geraldine

texted him to ask if they could meet outside Blackrock Library. When he got there, she said that she could no longer keep Thomas's secret because something about the old man scared her. She wanted to tell her gran, who would know how to organise medical help for him. Geraldine's words made sense but all day Shane had been thinking so obsessively about the well in Thomas's cellar that he couldn't think straight any more. Something snapped inside him now. He started to shout at Geraldine, using the same furious tone as his father used with his mother during their late-night rows.

Shane felt shocked at his own words, but a rage had taken possession of him. Insults tumbled out, the most bitter accusations. He found himself calling her a Judas and a traitor. Maybe a part of him had always been secretly jealous that Geraldine enjoyed such a happy home. But this could not explain his rage. He felt possessed by a panicked sense of terror that if anyone found out about Thomas's house before he got a chance to return there, he would throw away the only chance he had – no matter how unlikely or how superstitious – to make his parents stop arguing.

He wanted to stop shouting at Geraldine. He wanted to put his arms around her and apologise. But it was too late – she turned and ran away from him, down Newtown Avenue. Shane felt dizzy and scared. Nobody else was outside the closed library, but he did not feel alone. There was such an unnerving sensation of being watched that he began to run. He longed to chase after Geraldine, but an instinct – an overwhelmingly compulsive need – made him run towards Main Street. He reached the Rock Road and charged through the traffic in his haste to reach the house at the end of Castledawson Avenue.

A black cat scarpered from the wall as he climbed the front steps and pounded on the knocker. His parents would be furious at him for breaking in here. They would ground him in the Sion Hill duplex, which felt like a lonely prison. He kept knocking until he heard footsteps eventually descend the staircase. With a reluctant groan the rusty bolt was drawn back and a key clicked. The door creaked open a few inches. Thomas peered out.

'Geraldine is telling her gran about you,' Shane said. 'They're going to get you medical help.'

Thomas nodded slowly. 'I don't need help. I need to be left alone to die. But the night you broke in, I lost my chance.'

'Are you not scared to die?'

The old man looked out into the evening air. 'I have been scared to die many times. Each of us is scared when our time comes. We will do anything to cling on. People long for immortality – but immortality can be a lonesome, unnatural place.'

In the slanting sunlight Shane saw how sick Thomas looked. His eyes were exhausted, like he had not slept in years.

'Go away,' the old man said, starting to close the door. 'I am lonely, and loneliness is a dangerous condition. You don't belong here. Get the hell away.'

The heavy door was almost shut, but Thomas's hand shook so much that he seemed incapable of closing it those final few inches. He looked to be in pain. It seemed wrong to leave Thomas alone in agony, but Shane had more selfish reasons for wanting to stay.

'Let me in this last time,' he begged. 'I need to ask you one question.'

The old man hesitated as if battling with himself and then reluctantly opened the door. A tractor was cutting grass on the rugby pitch in the nearby college, but once Shane stepped into the hall, the sound seemed to come from another world. Thomas quickly closed the door and locked it.

'Ask your question and then go,' Thomas said. 'I am older and more exhausted than you could possibly imagine.'

Shane paused, feeling foolish. 'You said you made a wish in that cellar when you were a boy. You said it came true.'

The old man wearily sat on the stairs, shaking his head and muttering softly to himself. Eventually he looked up.

'I knew they had picked you the moment I saw you. They knew you wouldn't be able to resist the temptation.'

'Who are these people you keep talking about?'

Instead of replying the old man said, 'If you could have one wish, what would it be?'

'I asked you a question.'

'I asked you a better one. What is your heart's desire? When I was your age, only one living person knew that a well had been bricked up here – a mute named Joseph.'

'How did he know?'

'The longer you are forced to keep a secret, the heavier it becomes. What if, at the end of your life, you simply had to tell someone but wanted the secret to die with them? Who better to tell than a crippled mute boy who barely knew his alphabet? Joseph seemed the perfect choice to the dying man who had cut Michael Byrne's throat when he was a boy, because surely Joseph could never pass on the secret.'

Thomas rose. He seemed out of breath. Shane feared he would collapse.

'Older folk used to say that Michael Byrne should never have built his house over that well. Even in pagan times, its waters were rumoured to cure everything from blindness to croup. Pilgrims used to leave pieces of cloth tied to a crooked bush. Pilgrims could pray for their darkest wish here, but only a tiny few knew the price you had to pay to make a wish succeed.' Thomas sat wearily on the stairs. 'Go away, young O'Driscoll. You have your whole life ahead; that should be enough for anyone.'

'I can't listen to my parents argue anymore. If we had money they wouldn't argue.'

The old man looked up. 'Do you honestly believe money will make your parents happy?'

'It's what they argue over.'

'You don't know why they argue, what forces are playing with their thoughts.' The old man pointed to the locked door with his stick. 'Your grandfather was my friend once. He was the last real friend I ever had. For seventy years I've been unable to have friends; I have lived utterly alone. Now I'm telling you, on your grandfather's grave, open the door and get the hell away from this house.'

TWENTY-NINE

Joey

November 2009

On my first day in Stradbrook College, my greatest wish had been to be Shane's sidekick, but now, after glimpsing this wilder side of him on Bull Island, I no longer wished to become – as he called it – his blood brother. Instead I was starting to feel suffocated by always being in his shadow. I appreciated his friendship, but he was no longer the one whose company I wanted most. The person occupying my every waking thought was Geraldine.

I found it hard to sleep because so much was going on in my life and I had so many new emotions to cope with. I started to go for long walks at eleven o'clock every night. Mum didn't like it, but she let me go, knowing that otherwise I would sit up in my room for half the night, strumming my guitar and feeling caged. But often these walks only made me feel worse, because there seemed to be couples on every corner. I only had to turn onto Main Street from Brusna Cottages to spot cool-looking guys – those all-important two or three years older than me – venturing into the throbbing beat of The Wicked Wolf pub, leather jackets draped over one arm, gorgeous girls in party dresses on the other; guys with big jobs or rich daddies who seemed to personify the sense of money that flowed like electricity through Blackrock on such nights, when every girl looked chic and hot and every guy looked loaded and supremely confident.

Dad had purchased our small cottage for next to nothing before I was born. Brusna Cottages was dwarfed on every side by modern buildings. I had lived in Blackrock from birth, yet I felt that I didn't belong to it on those nightly walks up onto Temple Road, where I would pause to gaze in through the windows of Tonic bar and watch rich guys scoring rich girls, all hanging out together and laughing on the crowded leather sofas. This was the sort of place to which I wanted to bring Geraldine if I had the courage or the money. I had neither, and I knew that with Mum's job we were just about getting by financially until I could start earning too.

There were girls in my class that I could have asked out, but I only wanted Geraldine. She was the reason for my nightly walk further up Temple Road past the church and the Canada Life buildings to where it joined the dual carriageway and then back around by Newtown Avenue, which grew quiet after the bulk of traffic was siphoned off onto Seapoint Avenue.

I was generally alone with my thoughts when I reached the small cul-de-sac where Geraldine lived. I knew it was childish, but I loved the feel of being physically close to her for a few precious seconds before I headed for home. I would pause in the laneway opposite her house and gaze through the side gate into her garden where an old hammock swung. This seemed to me like the most magical spot on earth, although I'd have been mortified if Geraldine ever spotted me on this nightly pilgrimage that had become my unspoken gesture of love.

As I approached Geraldine's house on a Tuesday night, six days after our mid-term history exam, I became aware that someone was lurking in the small laneway opposite her home. I considered turning back, but curiosity or suspicion made me glance down the lane. It was dark, but I could make out a solitary figure, unaware of me as he stared wistfully up at Geraldine's lit bedroom window. At first I thought it was Shane, but when a shard of moonlight lit up the lane I recognised the old man who had harassed me outside my school. His face was haunting in its loneliness. He turned suddenly, as shocked to be discovered as I was to find him there. His aggression was gone. He looked vulnerable as he shuffled away down the lane on his walking stick, making his way onto Newtown Avenue. I followed him, feeling like a dog seeing another dog off his territory, although I had no right to stand outside Geraldine's house at night either. But he was so old that his presence there seemed utterly gross. I caught up with him on Newtown Avenue and grabbed his elbow.

'What were you doing back there?'

'Leave me alone.' He shrugged off my grip. 'You know nothing.'

'Stay away from Geraldine's house, you hear me?'

The old man stopped. 'Do you love her?'

'Mind your own business.' I knew I was blushing.

'If you love her, protect her from him. He steals everything.'

'You're talking nonsense. Tell me what Shane stole.'

'Come back to my house and I'll tell you everything.'

'I'm not going near your gaff. Tell me here.'

'You wouldn't believe me here. I leave a key above the back door. When you're ready to know the truth, pay me a visit. Until then, leave me alone in this purgatory.'

A passing car stopped, the driver unsure if I was harassing the old man. But Thomas ignored the man who called out. He walked off, leaning heavily on his stick, his face guarded beneath a black felt hat.

THIRTY

Shane

August 2007

All Shane needed to do was open the front door of Thomas's house and step outside into the safety of the evening air. But something made him hesitate. It was not just concern for Thomas, who looked gravely ill. It was an insatiable curiosity that kept tormenting him.

'Can you show me how to make a wish in that cellar?' he asked.

'One part of me longs to give you the chance,' Thomas whispered as he sat on the stairs. 'Another part of me is begging you to run away. You see, I don't know my own mind. Doctors always claimed I have a lot of split personalities.'

'What does that mean?'

'It means that I'm trying to hold out against myself.'

Shane's phone bleeped. He looked down. A text from Geraldine: *my gran phoned your dad. where u now?* When he looked up, Thomas's eyes were tightly closed as if trying to block something out.

'I was tricked into making a wish as a boy,' Thomas whispered. 'I refuse to trick you but I cannot stop you either. Only you can stop yourself. You will get your wish, you can be showered with money, but such wishes always come at a price.'

Something brushed against Shane's feet, startling him. It was the black cat he had seen on the wall, who had found its way in through the broken window. The cat sped off into the maze of deserted rooms. The temperature in the house seemed colder suddenly, the atmosphere more oppressive. 'I don't trust you,' he said, rattled. 'I don't like this place; I'm leaving now.'

Thomas's eyes snapped open. His face had changed during the few seconds when his eyes were closed. His features seemed distorted, his lips covered in froth. Giving a snort like a pig, he rose from the stairs and shuffled towards the boy. At first Shane couldn't make out what he was saying because the words had started to come in a strangulated grunt. Only when Thomas repeated them did it sound like his own voice. Even then it was barely above a whisper. 'I need my painkillers. Fetch a glass of water from the kitchen tap. Quick, lad, don't tarry; this pain is killing me.'

Thomas looked to be in such agony that the boy reluctantly went down into the kitchen. The only drinking glass was caked in dust and he needed to clean it with his shirt. He filled it with oily tap water. When he turned around, Thomas was standing directly behind him. The old man grabbed the glass and swallowed two blue tablets. He grimaced, his voice harsh.

'I've not tasted viler water since the Eagle Tavern.

Make your decision, boy. Time is running out. Your father will never let you return here.' Thomas stepped closer. 'He knows not to trust strangers, especially a coward who is afraid to die.'

Shane backed away. 'I've told you, I'm leaving.'

'The moment you broke in, I knew they had summoned you. You are not the boy they wanted, though. They have already killed his father in a car crash up at the Hellfire Club, with music blaring from the tangled wreckage. But they are running out of time. So even though you're weak, you're the boy they'll settle for.'

Shane's phone beeped again. He glanced down. Another text from Geraldine: *tell me where u are. am worried.* He tried to text back, but when he pressed the keys on his phone, the battery died.

'You think you can leave, but you can't,' Thomas added. 'Greed and curiosity have you hooked.'

'I can leave here whenever I want,' Shane snapped, rattled. 'You're crazy.'

'Am I? I'm a gambling man; I gambled my way through several fortunes between dice and cards and hounds. I wager that you haven't got the guts to call my bluff and find out if I am lying about that cellar.'

Shane stepped back, relieved to feel the handle of the back door behind him. He was almost out of there. He looked up to see the black cat perched on an empty shelf, observing them with bored eyes.

'That's right, leave by the back door.' Thomas's tone became haughty, snidely demeaning. 'That's the door reserved for servants like the penniless skivvying girl your grandmother was. You O'Driscolls were always peasants with no class. Run away home to your pathetic failure of a father.'

'Don't call him that!' Shane said angrily.

'How pathetic to try to hobnob with the quality in Sion Hill when he hasn't two pennies to rub together. You O'Driscolls were always dirt-poor, breeding like rabbits in the mud cabins on this avenue until the Holy Ghost fathers could no longer stand the stench of poverty wafting over their wall. Geraldine has ten times more courage than you.'

'Leave Geraldine out of this!'

Shane could hardly believe that this was the same soft-spoken man they had befriended a few nights before.

'You were never good enough to be her friend. Now, run off back to your penniless, bickering parents.'

Shane only needed to open the back door and scramble his way up through those bushes. The groundsman would still be cutting grass in the college, cars still busily passing the railings on the Rock Road. But the taunts about his parents rankled too much.

'I'm not scared of you, you twisted old snob. I'll go down into that cellar and prove you're telling a pack of lies.'

The cat made a lunge down onto the floor and darted away. The malice left Thomas's face, the snarling anger draining from his body. His eyes became indescribably sad.

'Sometimes I can't control the spiteful things I say,' he said softly. 'Think carefully before you do this.'

But Shane didn't want to think carefully. He would show the last of the McCormack family that the O'Driscolls were no cowards and then he would leave this house forever. He entered the passageway. The cellar was in darkness, but the exposed water possessed a shimmer of its own.

'How badly do you want to be rich?' Thomas's voice came from behind him, tinged with regret.

'Just tell me what to do and let's get this nonsense finished.'

'Take the black-handled knife from the water. Remove the dice too.'

Shane knelt. He had never known water to feel this cold.

'Hand me the knife,' Thomas ordered.

'What are you going to do with it?'

'Just give it here. I was a good man once; I even planned to be a priest.' Thomas looked down at the knife Shane handed him. 'You might be wise to throw those dice into a gutter. They never brought me luck, in this life or any other.'

Shane felt scared but his pride was still hurt by the comments about his parents.

'My grandad always called your mother a fearsome, bitter snob.' As he looked down, Shane remembered with a sense of horror that the dice in his palm were made out of bone, discoloured over the centuries.

'You are holding the relics of St Mochanna,' Thomas said. 'Those relics were in the Dawson family for generations. On her deathbed, Henry Dawson's mother placed them in a locket around his neck and begged him to keep them safe. I still remember the feel of that locket around my neck. I remember her dying and how unprepared I was to inherit the family estates. I was a young fool; I was debauched by grief; I was led astray by rakes.'

'What are you talking about?'

'I'm talking about having nothing else left to gamble with. I'm talking about waking up alone in the Hellfire Club to find my fellow rakes gone. I'm talking about a black cat changing shape and becoming a man, if you can call the devil a man. He blew on those relics softly and handed them back to me – reshaped, he said, to better reflect my damaged soul. The devil wagered my soul – the soul of Henry Dawson – against all the other souls that I might bring into his web, in time. He said it would amuse him to see good and bad souls battle for supremacy in the turmoil inside me.'

'You are truly insane,' Shane said. 'And I don't believe that these are the bones of any saint.'

'You're right. That monk was a coward, afraid to face his God. He made a pact with the devil and got his wish of continued life. He was found dead in the rushlight of his cell, with a young novice kneeling beside him, shaking and holding a blood-stained knife like he didn't know how it got there.'

'You're a fantasist … a lunatic … a liar.'

'Then leave this cellar.'

'I'll leave when I'm good and ready.'

Shane was trembling. He wanted to leave: every nerve end within him ached to do so, yet he found that he couldn't leave. Curiosity had him gripped. The thought of holding human bones repulsed him. He wanted to throw them away, yet he also longed to make a wish. This old man was deluded, yet just maybe, if he did make a wish, his parents' luck might change – one of them might buy a winning lottery scratch card or get a promotion at work. He didn't care how it happened, once there was enough money to stop the endless arguments at home. Closing his eyes, he tossed the dice into the water. 'Make me rich,' he whispered fervently. 'Whatever it takes, make me rich.'

The splash came as if from a great distance. Then Shane's eyes opened in fear as Thomas's left hand gripped his wrist. The old man's clasp was fierce, as if summoning every last ounce of strength. With his right hand, Thomas nicked Shane's palm with the black-handled knife, then sliced open his own palm to let blood flow between the two wounds.

'We're blood brothers now, young O'Driscoll,' he said, 'for all eternity.' He plunged their hands into the water. 'There are always two wishes: the second wish belongs to me and to all the lost souls gathered inside me.'

THIRTY-ONE

Joey

November 2009

Meet please 4 just 1 date any time or place. I pressed send on my phone and prayed that – like most of the class – Geraldine kept her mobile on silent. It was the morning after I had confronted that old man outside her house. We had a half-day on Wednesdays and business studies was my final class. It was my only subject that Shane didn't take and Geraldine was always more relaxed in it because he was not in the classroom. I saw her glance at her phone, half-concealed amid the books on her desk. She brushed back her hair, aware that I was watching, but made no effort to text back a reply.

Our business studies teacher asked me a simple question and got annoyed when I couldn't answer. But I found it impossible to concentrate on anything with Geraldine this close. I had to endure the agony of waiting for a response until we found ourselves shoulder to shoulder, filing out into the noisy corridor.

'I've told you, Joey, I don't do dates. Lots of girls would be thrilled skinny if you asked them out, girls who need a guy to dangle on their arm like a trophy. Pick any girl you like and I'll even ask her for you.'

'I can do my own asking,' I said stubbornly. 'I'm asking you.'

To my surprise, she blushed suddenly. 'And you have a special way of asking. I'm impressed. It's like you know me inside out.'

We reached the glass doors leading outside. Shane was there, waiting for me.

'I can't talk with him about.' Geraldine lowered her voice. 'If we bumped into each other by fluke in the shopping centre this afternoon it wouldn't be a date, just a co-incidence. Promise you won't tell Shane.'

Geraldine brushed past me and out the glass doors, ignoring Shane. He scrutinised me as I emerged.

'What's the story?' he asked. 'Do you fancy a frame of snooker later? Maybe get the dart to Dún Laoghaire and chill out?'

'Sorry, Shane, I've got things to do.'

'Savage; go you.' Shane grinned but something about his eyes perturbed me. I was halfway home before I realised where I knew that look from: his gaze mirrored the same loneliness I had glimpsed in the old man's eyes. I hadn't time to dwell on this because I needed to get home and raid my excuse for a wardrobe. I tried on various T-shirts, trying to look cool and failing miserably. I combed my hair forward and then brushed it back with my fingers. One way made me look dumb, the other way dumber. But I didn't really care what I looked like, because I was buzzing at the thought of meeting Geraldine.

When I reached Blackrock Shopping Centre there was

no sign of Geraldine. I sat on a bench on the open air concourse on the lower level, so busy watching the door onto Main Street that I never realised she was leaning over the balcony above me until I felt an M&M strike my forehead. When I glanced up, she grinned and disappeared. I bounded up the escalator to the upper level and she was already slipping down the stairs on the far side. I needed to backtrack and was breathless by the time I caught up with her, leaning against the stones of the ornate flowerbed.

'What's an ig?' she asked.

'Tell me.'

'An Eskimo's house without a loo.'

'That's the worst joke I ever heard.'

'Trust me, I have a hundred worse ones.'

'I'm glad I caught up with you, so.'

'You couldn't catch a cold,' she teased. 'That's what I like about you.'

'That's not nice.' I made a hurt face.

'Bring me for a walk and I'll be nice to you.' She headed for the entrance. 'I only mean that you're not sly.'

'Is that meant as a compliment?'

'It's meant as a fact. Like the fact that you have surprisingly romantic qualities.'

'Such as?'

'Don't be so coy, you know well what I mean. It's just a pity you let Shane walk all over you.'

'Can we stop mentioning Shane?'

'Gladly.' We stepped out onto Main Street. 'This afternoon, your wish is my command. And if you really want me to show you the places that are most special to me, then that is what I'm going to do.'

Something about her remark perturbed me, but I wasn't going to let it disturb the joy of finally being alone with her. I had known the streets of Blackrock all my life, but wandering through them with Geraldine added a new magic to them. We talked about people in our class and what books we loved and what music we enjoyed downloading and what it felt like to be an only child, living with one parent – or, in her case, one grandparent. It wasn't a date because we were just wandering up George's Avenue and coming back by Carysfort, but it felt more special than any night out in Tonic or The Wicked Wolf. Finally, I suggested a coffee in Starbucks in the old post office on Main Street. At the counter, I grabbed our two cappuccinos before she could object to me paying for them and walked through the back of the shop, out onto the veranda that overlooked the DART station and the derelict Blackrock Baths. When I looked back, Geraldine was hesitating in the doorway.

'Is out here OK?' I asked. 'I thought you'd like to be in the air.'

'I do like being outside,' she said, 'It's just …' She sat down at a table and stared towards the sea. 'It's nothing really; it's probably time I grew up, I guess.'

'I don't understand.'

'I've always avoided this view, because my mum died swimming in that bay.'

'I'm sorry. Do you want to go back inside?'

'No. I need to stop being so superstitious. As a kid, I kept all my precious possessions locked in a treasure box where I knew they'd be safe. For the past two years I've kinda locked myself away in a box too, in case I get hurt again.'

'I'd never hurt you, Geraldine.'

She took a sip of her coffee. 'Tell me how you know so much about my feelings.'

'What makes you think I do?'

She looked past me out towards the sea. Her hair was beautiful in the sunlight. 'You just do.'

'I know you're cool … and drop-dead gorgeous, by the way.'

'And I know you're a bit of a sap.'

'Thanks a lot.' I pretended to look hurt again.

'Not in a bad sense. You're a nice, somewhat handsome sap.'

'So, can we go on a proper date?'

'I've told you; I'm not ready to date anyone yet.'

'Then let me be around you as a friend. I love being near you.'

Geraldine glanced around as if fearful of being observed. She lowered her voice. 'I could use someone around me. It's crazy, Joey, but for two years I was scared without knowing why. Then, on the morning Shane walked into our classroom, I knew what I had always been scared of – that he would come back to get me.'

'In what way could Shane get you?'

'There's something unnatural about him. I feel I'm constantly being watched. Even at night, I sense Shane keeping tabs on me.'

'Maybe it's not Shane.'

'What do you mean?'

I hesitated. 'I think it's that old man, Thomas.'

Caution entered Geraldine's voice. 'What do you know about Thomas? He should be dead long ago; they only gave him months to live.' She was silent for a moment, lost in thought. Then her fingers reached across the table to entwine with mine. 'It scares me that I like you this much, Joey. You see, I liked a boy like this before and he changed. Promise you won't change.'

'How did Shane change?'

'I wish I knew.' Geraldine untwined her fingers and rose to stand at the railings. 'I wish I could explain it.'

THIRTY-TWO

Geraldine

August 2007

At two o'clock in the morning, the police car stopped outside the unlit house at the end of Castledawson Avenue. In the back seat, Geraldine sat between her gran and Shane's father. The man looked shattered as he stared out the window. He had become increasingly agitated since Geraldine mentioned a well in the cellar, questioning her so intensely that her gran made him stop because he was upsetting the girl.

Geraldine wasn't sure if the police believed her story about an old man living here. At first they said that it was too early to talk about Shane being a missing person – he was probably just out late somewhere with a friend. But Geraldine knew that Shane had no friends in Blackrock except her. She also knew that they had ceased to be mere friends and had become something more. Only now, when Shane was missing, could she admit to herself that she loved him. This was what had made his earlier tirade of insults outside the library so hard to bear. It was like a force he could not control had gripped him. This made her scared for him.

'We need to climb the wall,' she told the two policemen

getting out of the car. 'I can squeeze in the window and open the back door.'

But they ignored her, climbing the steps to bang on the front door, even though she insisted that Thomas would not answer. She had never known any night to be so silent, as if the darkness itself was alert and listening to their pounding. Then the policemen came back down the steps to get equipment to force open the lock. As the wood began to splinter, Shane's father called his son's name repeatedly. Finally the lock gave way and the heavy door swung open. The policeman shone their torches into the dark hall.

'There's no one inside this house or they would have come down,' Shane's dad insisted, almost as if trying to convince himself. 'We've made enough noise to waken the dead.'

Even the policemen seemed reluctant to step inside. There was something oppressive about the darkness, something that chilled them to the bone. Then, from the shadows, there came a movement. Shane's father called his son's name, but it was a stray cat that shot past them and out the front door.

Geraldine couldn't wait any longer. She needed to find out if Shane was all right. Instinctively, she ran down the back steps towards the kitchen, with her gran shouting at her to come back and Shane's father again calling his name. The policemen were trying to keep up with her or at least to shine some light on the stairs so that she wouldn't fall. Geraldine entered the kitchen and stopped because the room felt so cold. The four adults crowded down the stairs behind her, more living souls than had set foot inside that house for years.

'There's no one down here,' a policeman told her. 'You go back up with your grandmother and wait in the car. I promise we'll go through every room, just in case.'

He shone his torch around the kitchen to show it was empty. He was about to turn away when Geraldine screamed.

'What's wrong?' he asked.

'Shine it over in the corner again. On the door frame.'

At first the policeman didn't know what she meant. Then he lowered the beam so that it lit up the base of the open doorway that led to the cellar. Geraldine's gran tried to hold her but she was already running forward to where the torchlight picked up four fingertips clinging to the doorframe. Someone had collapsed in the passageway, frantically trying to reach the kitchen, and clung to the doorframe while another person tried to drag him back.

Geraldine knelt beside the arrayed fingers; telling Shane that he was now safe as she went to unclench them. Then she took her hand away from the fingers in shock because they did not belong to the boy. It was Thomas who had been trying to clutch onto the doorframe when he collapsed. His face looked petrified. When the policemen shone their torches down the passageway she saw Shane's body behind his, also unconscious, as if Shane had fallen and banged his head. But Shane had not been trying to flee from the cellar. His arms were locked around the old man's legs in a desperate rugby tackle, like he had been trying to haul him back down into that cellar or to retrieve something stolen from him.

THIRTY-THREE

Joey

November 2009

I walked over to stand beside Geraldine on the veranda of Starbucks. She looked at me.

'We found Shane and Thomas unconscious in that old house,' she said. 'For three days both were in a coma in Vincent's Hospital, like boxers who'd knocked each other out. Seeing Shane attached to a drip was horrible.'

I put my arm around her and Geraldine told me things she had never talked about to a living soul. About how Shane's body had been unmarked except for a bruise on his forehead, but the doctors were unsure whether he would regain consciousness or – if he did – whether he would be mentally impaired. Every night Thomas's pulse dipped so low that he seemed certain to die. Whenever this happened, Shane's pulse would also dip, though nobody could explain why a healthy boy was hovering at death's door.

'I blamed myself,' Geraldine said. 'Shane was a bit of a wimp but he followed me into that house.'

'You've nothing to blame yourself for,' I said. 'Shane survived.'

Geraldine looked up. 'It sounds crazy, Joey, but I don't know if he did.'

'What do you mean?'

'After three days he woke. He looked OK, apart from his eyes … they seemed older, like they didn't belong to him any more. His parents brought him home. But something must have affected his brain when he fell because, when I visited him, he was different from the boy I'd loved.'

'What happened to Thomas?'

'He woke from his coma on the same day Shane woke. He started raving. He turned out to have had a history of mental illness, delusions, paranoid schizophrenia. He kept turning up at my door, making bizarre claims. Gran wouldn't let him near me. Then a truly freaky thing happened.'

'What?'

Geraldine looked out at the bay. 'Shane's folks were becoming famous in Sion Hill for their quarrels. But the neighbours had never heard any row to match the one on the evening when Shane and his dad came home to find Thomas sitting with his mum in their kitchen. The woman had flipped with stress and kept shouting that Thomas was her real son. Apparently Shane grabbed a kitchen knife to try and stab Thomas and Shane's dad was trying to keep them apart and to throw Thomas out and stop his wife from following him. The neighbours say she kept screaming that she wouldn't spend another night under the same roof as Shane.' Geraldine looked at me. 'That was the night the duplex went up in flames; the night Shane's dad carried his wife's body outside, then ran back in, thinking he needed to save his son.' She shivered. 'I think Shane started that fire to kill them both.'

'That's crazy talk,' I said.

A group of girls came out onto the balcony with their coffees, chatting loudly.

'I don't trust him,' Geraldine said in a low voice. 'He wanted to be rich. He is now; he inherited a fortune. He gets whatever he wants. He wants to find a way to get me. Is he using you, Joey?'

'No one is using me,' I said. 'I'm just myself.'

'A big romantic sap.' Geraldine leaned forward and kissed me suddenly on the lips. 'That's to say thank you – nobody else ever wrote a poem for me before.'

'What do you mean, before?'

Geraldine's smile started to grow anxious. 'Before you dropped a poem in my letterbox last night. The poem about longing to walk with me in Blackrock and share all the places I love …' Her smile was replaced by a puzzled stare. 'How did you manage to list so many places that are special to me, like you already knew all my secrets?'

'I never wrote you any poem.'

'It was signed in your name, in perfect copperplate handwriting.' Geraldine stepped back, scared. 'We're letting him do this; we're letting Shane manipulate us.'

'Geraldine, listen to me …'

But Geraldine didn't listen. She ran back through the café. The girls at the other table stopped their chatter to stare at me as if I had done something terrible. I ran after her, but by the time I got out onto Main Street Geraldine was gone. I stood there, feeling confused and angry, but most of all feeling the sweet aftertaste of her kiss.

THIRTY-FOUR

Joey

November 2009

Before that kiss in Starbucks Geraldine had felt untouchable, but now she was flesh and blood that I longed to kiss again. Somebody was playing mind games with us, but I couldn't be certain whether Shane or the old man had written that poem in my name. When I had disturbed Thomas outside Geraldine's house, could he have already posted it in her letterbox, malevolently meddling in other people's lives?

On Thursday in school, Shane knew that something was wrong because Geraldine studiously avoided me. Looking around the class and remembering being bullied in my former school, I couldn't stop wondering if any of my classmates were laughing at my expense, having composed the poem between them as a joke. I couldn't stop such wild speculation because I had no one to confide in. I didn't know whether to trust Shane any more, yet he was the only person I could go to for advice, because he felt like my only real friend in school. This was because he never allowed me the chance to get friendly with anyone else. If I started a conversation with someone, Shane always contrived to join in, so that they wound up talking to him instead. Shane and I were inseparable in people's eyes, but only because he had started to dominate every aspect of my school life.

When Shane asked me how I had spent Wednesday afternoon I dodged the question by telling him about the old demo tapes Bongo Drums had in his attic. Shane was adamant that I should ask Bongo for them. He claimed that my mum would give anything to hear Dad's voice again. But what if his songs failed to match the status I had granted them in my mind? I decided to seek Mum's advice on Thursday evening.

'Mum, a teacher in school has old tapes of Dad in his attic.'

Mum looked up from her crossword. 'How come?'

'He was a drummer in the sessions. The thing is, I didn't know if you'd want to hear his voice again.'

Mum put down the book. 'I often hear his voice,' she said. 'I hear him sometimes in how you talk and always in how you laugh.'

'That's not the same thing.'

'Who is this teacher?'

'Mr Quinn. Bongo Drums, we call him.'

'Bongo Drums.' She laughed. 'That's a good name for Ben Quinn. I remember him on the road. He had a droopy moustache and a fondness for German women. He could talk the hind legs off a donkey.' She reached across for my hand. 'If Ben has tapes, you don't need my permission to listen to them.'

'I'd like us to listen to them together.'

Mum shook her head. 'Your father's songs are still too raw for me, Joey. I went through a lot of grief around the time he died; I had demons I needed to confront. I'm getting on with my life now.' She picked up her book. 'You listen to the tapes, but do it on your headphones in your room where I can't overhear. I don't ask much, Joey, but promise to keep them away from me.'

Mum looked jaded after her day's work. She worked overtime every Saturday to bring home extra money. I was always offering to get a part-time job to help out, but she didn't want anything to distract me from my studies. Seeing her tired face, I felt a sense of responsibility to make something good of my life to compensate for her years of struggling to bring me up alone. Shane joked glibly about me cutting loose into music and him becoming my manager and organising gigs on a tour of cities I'd barely heard of. But a family only has room for one dreamer. Dad had already used up all our dreams. I was passionate about music, but when the time came I would study accountancy or business, any steady career that guaranteed a regular wage. It was the least I owed Mum. I went back to my homework, deciding to tell Bongo Drums to keep his tapes. That would allow me to keep alive the illusion of Dad's brilliance in my mind without having to discover just how good or bad he really was.

When I mentioned this to Shane on Friday morning he grew annoyed, saying I was making a coward's decision. However I was increasingly suspicious about Shane's motives. Geraldine kept ignoring my texts, but finally I gave Shane the slip for long enough to sneak a few words with her in the corridor.

'Meet me alone,' I said, 'for five minutes, anywhere.'

Geraldine looked over my shoulder. 'Your shadow is chasing you. We're never alone, Joey. I'm being drawn into something I don't understand. I feel I'm being watched.'

I silently cursed as Shane approached.

'Maybe it's not Shane,' I whispered.

'What do you mean?'

Before I could reply, Shane had reached us. Geraldine hugged her books to her chest and walked away. Shane barged against my shoulder good-naturedly.

'So, what's the story?' he asked. 'Have you a date or what?'

'Why don't you get a life of your own, Shane, and keep your nose out of mine?'

He laughed at my outburst. 'Calm down, Joey, true love is never smooth. I'm just saying I wouldn't kick that girl out of bed for getting crumbs on my pillow.'

He grinned and kept grinning until he had coaxed a half-hearted smile from me. I was in no mood for Shane, but it was hard to stay angry for long in his company when he had a different personality to suit every occasion. Yet behind the sardonic grin I was starting to sense a desperate loneliness within him. Still, maybe Geraldine had no reason to be so scared of Shane, because maybe the person playing games with all our lives was that old man on Castledawson Avenue. I could only find out by confronting him.

THIRTY-FIVE

Joey

November 2009

O n Friday night I told Mum I was taking my usual walk. But instead, I crossed the Rock Road and slipped down Castledawson Avenue to the house where Thomas was said to live. The windows were dark; the rooms, abandoned-looking. The door knocker was loud, yet no footsteps came down the hall in reply to my knocking. I climbed onto the wall and was lit up by the security lights of the Blackrock Clinic before I jumped down into the darkness of the garden, where bushes guarded the slope leading to the kitchen. I was covered in scratches by the time I managed to find the key that Thomas had mentioned.

Opening the back door and entering the kitchen, I tried to imagine Shane and Geraldine here two years before. I could see the outline of a flight of stairs. I needed to duck under thick clouds of cobwebs to reach them. Sections of banisters were missing, as if someone had kicked them to smithereens. The faintest glow of streetlight came from a fanlight above the front door in the hallway. I entered a back room with its fireplace torn out. There was a mattress on the floor, a few blankets and a table with a chipped mug and a loaf of bread. I sensed myself being watched and turned to see the old man behind me.

'Did curiosity overcome you, or has he sent you to do his dirty work?'

'Nobody sent me,' I replied. 'I came to tell you to stop causing trouble.'

'Trouble?' The old man laughed bitterly. 'My troubles only started when he barged into my life. Did you tell him I want it back?'

'What do you want back?'

The old man approached. Every time he took a step I took a step back.

'Are you so dumb you can't guess? I mean, just how clueless are you, Joey?'

I could retreat no further. I was pressed against a wall coated in mould. Beside me a thick blanket covered the window.

'I want to know if you sent Geraldine a poem in my name. I want you to stay out of our lives.'

'You want more than that, Joey. You wish to know what all this is about. Curiosity is a dangerous disease. Be careful or you might get your wish. Did he send you?'

'Nobody sent me.'

'Are you sure? He has subtle ways of making people do his bidding. He has business to conclude in this house but is too afraid to set foot inside this door. You tell him the last will and testament of Thomas McCormack is hidden here. It leaves everything to the boy who befriended a dying man. If he wants this house, to go with the other riches he keeps inheriting, tell him to come here in person and find the will. Otherwise, when the blasted, ramshackle body I'm forced to occupy finally gives out, the solicitors will follow the instructions in the original will to supervise the demolition of this house, brick by brick, and sell the site to developers. He pines for his old home here, just like he used to pine to own Castledawson House after he gambled it away. Tell him he can have his house back if he comes here. He just needs to kill me first.'

'What do you mean, "if he wants his house back"? It's your house. Why would you leave it to him?'

'I possess nothing, Joey, not even a family now. My parents died in a fire. My aunt crashed her car in England when she realised she was living with a changeling. I only ever had one true friend – a girl I still love.'

'You're insane,' I said. 'Your two brothers went mad here too.'

The old man pressed his face to mine. 'I am an only child, four months older than you.'

I pushed him back, very gently. He seemed so frail I was afraid he would fall.

'There's medication you should be on.'

He lifted his stick and scattered the crockery on the table. 'I don't need medication! I need you to believe me. That changeling stole my life! And before that, he stole other lives. A line of old men stretching back across the centuries have been found with their throats cut after he had finally finished using the bodies he stole from them as boys.' He looked at me. 'Do you want to live forever, Joey?'

'Doesn't everyone?'

'Not everyone gets the chance. But suppose you were given a chance to never die? What if your soul and your thoughts could live on – not inside your own body because all bodies wear out, but with other souls inside a fresh body? What would you do if offered this chance of immortality?'

I edged towards the door. The old man sat down, wearily.

'I don't blame you for not believing me. Even my own mother didn't recognise me at first. When she did, he killed her in the fire.' He stared at his gnarled fingers. 'You and I should be classmates, Joey.'

'You need help,' I said, 'you're schizophrenic.'

'I need that changeling to cut my throat. Then at least I would be set free from his old body so that my soul could merge with his soul back inside my own body. He tried to do it two years ago – the night I clung to the doorframe; the night he slipped and banged his skull. If he had succeeded, our souls would still be locked in combat, but inside one body – not split in two like this. As it is, I am like his shadow and he is like mine. Imagine how it feels, Joey, to see someone else walk around inside your own body? I know his every thought. He is weary of being condemned to live each lifetime alone. He wants companionship, but I'm the one creature on earth who understands him. The voices whispering in his head keep urging him to kill me and safeguard their secret. But he is too scared of being left utterly alone.'

He placed his head in his hands. I edged closer to the door.

'Ask yourself, Joey – if he is a natural being, why is Geraldine so scared in his presence? She can sense evil.' He looked up. 'Stay and listen to me because you and I both love the same girl.'

'Leave Geraldine alone, do you hear?'

'She is in mortal danger. He is using you like bait to lead her to him. My real name is Shane O'Driscoll. You must believe this fact and make Geraldine believe it too. Tell her that inside this wasted body I am still the boy she loved. Tell her I am writing down a word here because she and I swore never to say it aloud to another living soul.'

He scribbled the word Concord on a scrap of paper and handed it to me.

'What does Concord mean?' I asked.

'Ask her.' He watched carefully to ensure I put it in my pocket. 'Have you ever seen pictures of a tornado? It begins small, just a whipped-up breeze. Then it sucks up everything in its path until it becomes a pillar of cloud, feeding off its own momentum. Inside his head, there exists a tornado of voices. He has a jigsaw of lost souls jostling inside him. I can hear an echo of them inside my head too. A hunchback mute thought that he could save their souls by merging them with the soul of a boy destined for the priesthood. But Thomas could never grant them absolution. He tried to lock himself away and die unnoticed but the whisperers knew that he could be tempted. They chose their victim badly this time. Tell the changeling I want my life back. Tell him to put an end to my purgatory, here in his house where it all went wrong. Only one of us was meant to live after that night. Tell him I'm waiting for him to slit my throat like he once slit the throats of pigs for the nuns.'

THIRTY SIX

Thomas

December 2006

At one time the windows on this asylum in New Jersey had bars across them. Thomas feels certain of this, though he might be getting it confused with a different asylum. There have been so many asylums and homeless shelters that they have all come to look alike. The glass in this window is reinforced, but with a hammer, you could smash it and escape back into the world.

Not that Thomas wishes to escape. His health is failing and it is below zero outside. For seven decades he has been blown across America like a piece of tumbleweed. Sometimes, doctors quiz him about the cities he has lived in and the jobs he worked at. Slaughterhouses and abattoirs, he tells them, he was especially good with pigs. Pigs trusted him. Thomas doesn't trust doctors, however. Doctors are always trying to get patients to talk. Thomas doesn't want to talk. Death is coming and he wants to be left alone at this window to gaze out at the snow.

In the ward behind him, fellow patients doze in chairs or stare into space. Many have no idea why they are here. Thomas is here because his bones cannot survive another winter sleeping on the streets. He is too old to cope with crack addicts kicking at the cardboard he tries to wrap himself in at night. Nothing blocks the wind like cardboard, but nothing dissolves so quickly in the rain. Living on the streets was easier when people were crazy with drink or plain crazy. Thomas had coped back then, because any lunatic can be quietened if something human remains in their souls. Thomas understands souls; Thomas can see the pain in strangers' souls. Thomas has soothed them like you soothe a scared pig. But today's crack addicts are different, because drugs have stolen their souls. Crack addicts would feel no remorse about killing him, because they would not remember doing so afterwards.

Therefore, last month, when a cop car slowed down outside the warehouse where Thomas was trying to sleep in the doorway, he had pretended to be crazy. Cops always get nervous in case an old man dies in custody, leaving them with mountains of paperwork. Thomas had known that they would bring him to an asylum. This asylum has no straitjackets or electric shock treatment. It is like a five-star hotel, where lunch is served with injections. His fellow patients are sensitive, damaged people who hear imaginary voices, or else conmen who have learned how to fake mental illness in winter by pretending to hear voices. Thomas keeps himself to himself, because he is as sane as the conmen but he really can hear voices.

Nothing can stop those voices. For months they have been whispering, 'Take us home.' Over the decades he has tried losing himself in the oblivion of drink or backbreaking labour. He has tried losing himself in religion with manic-eyed preachers, but the best he has managed is to learn to stop replying to their urgent pleas.

So when a voice calls his name now as he sits at the window, it takes Thomas a moment to realise that it does not come from his head. He becomes aware of two men behind him. They are not patients, because they stand with too much authority. They cannot be nurses, because he isn't due medication. They cannot be visitors, because nobody ever visits him. Therefore they must be doctors, and doctors mean trouble. Last week, a doctor had examined Thomas and told him his cancer was so advanced that he only had six months left to live. The doctor had talked about a programme of pain relief when the end came, but Thomas has no intention of still being in this asylum then. When spring comes, he will find somewhere to die under the stars. He only wants two types of dealings with doctors: to convince them he is mad at the onset of winter, and to convince them he has regained his sanity each spring.

'Thomas McCormack?' the man asks again.

Thomas decides to play dumb. The snow outside the window looks deep. He will die of exposure if they evict him.

'Are you Thomas McCormack from Ireland?' Thomas hunches his shoulders. If they don't leave him alone, he may need to bite one of them. A padded cell is no place to spend Christmas, but at least he will survive there, unlike on a park bench.

'Thomas McCormack from Castledawson Avenue in Blackrock: youngest son of the late Mrs Margaret McCormack and brother to the late Francis and Peter McCormack?'

The shock of hearing these names is so great that Thomas looks up. He recognises one man as a doctor, but the second man is a stranger, and certainly no doctor in such an expensive business suit. He is too well dressed to be an ordinary cop. Perhaps they have sent a commissioner to arrest him.

'Are Frankie and Pete dead?'

The well-dressed man sits beside Thomas, unable to disguise his excitement. 'So you are the Thomas McCormack I'm seeking?'

'I asked you a question,' Thomas says.

'Both your brothers died some years ago.'

'They lived to be old men,' Thomas says. 'You took your time finding me, Mister.'

The man nods. 'I've been searching for quite a while.'

'And I've been in hiding for quite a while,' Thomas replies. 'Seventy years – I've already served a life sentence, but I knew you cops would find me. I've known it since the night I left Joseph's body on the rocks at Blackrock House. Bring me a pen, Mister, and I'll sign my confession to murder.'

The two men look at one another. 'Whose murder did you commit?'

Thomas sighs. 'Don't play games with me, Mister, and I won't play games with you. I slit the throat of a hunchbacked mute with a black-handled knife for a crime done to me. Is it a crime to want your own body back? I had endured four years of deformity, four years of sleeping beside squealing pigs and being forced to work for the nuns in Sion Hill. I watched a changeling usurp my place and enter a seminary as if he was a devout young man. I lured him out from that seminary. I provoked and provoked him until he stabbed me. I made him so angry that he forgot he was really stabbing his former self. The pain was terrible but I found myself freed from his old body and back inside my former skin. But I wasn't free of him: his voice and the others have been like a virus in my bloodstream ever since. I could have returned to the seminary but I knew I was damned and so I administered to the damned. I whispered the last rites in roadside ditches and flea-bed dosshouses. I did God's work in my own way, as a spoiled priest who brought disgrace to my mother by disappearing. That's who I murdered, Mister. Now ship me home to Ireland and, if cancer doesn't kill me first, I'll happily hang for my crime.'

THIRTY-SEVEN

Joey

November 2009

Ibarely slept on the Friday night. When I did, I had strange dreams in which Shane and Thomas became jumbled up. I woke up drenched in sweat, convinced I had been awoken by a desperate squeal for mercy. The only sound in my bedroom was the ticking clock, but I was certain the cry had been real. I didn't know if it came from a pig or a human being. I couldn't shake off this sense of foreboding or bear to be alone in my room. I stood outside my mum's door, wanting to turn the handle. But I was too old to disturb her, and how could I explain what troubled me? She was surprised to find me sitting in the kitchen when she got up early for work.

'Is something wrong?' She looked worried. 'You know I'm always here if you need advice.'

'I'm fine,' I lied. 'I just slept badly.'

She was gone then, rushing off to work. I tidied up the house and thought of going to see Shane. But the old man's words made no sense in the light of day. The person I wanted to talk to was Geraldine. I kept texting her, but got no reply until I sent one that read: *What does the word*

Concord mean? A reply came: *Meet u at Idrone Terrace 4pm.* I
went to sit on the bench overlooking the sea at Idrone
Terrace an hour early because I felt uneasy sitting alone at
home. It felt like some presence was watching me there.
Geraldine looked concerned when she finally arrived and
saw me.

'Are you OK?'

'I'm freaked out,' I said.

'What's happened?' She sat beside me on the bench.

'You know how you feel you're being watched?'
Geraldine nodded.

'The night that poem was posted through your letterbox, I saw somebody outside your house. But it wasn't
Shane, it was Thomas.'

She shivered, 'Even thinking about Thomas makes my
skin crawl.'

'I visited his house last night. He claims to be watching
over you to protect you. He made all kinds of mad claims.'

'Like what?'

Geraldine was silent as I repeated most of what
Thomas had said. By the time I finished I felt foolish for
having ever taken his words seriously.

'I still have nightmares about his house,' Geraldine said
after a while. 'God forgive me, but I wish he would die
and someone would knock it down. He's insane. But the
odd thing is that if what he said was true, everything else
would fall into place.'

'It can't be true,' I said.

'Well, obviously not.' Geraldine laughed nervously. 'I
mean, it would be just too weird.'

We sat in silence for a moment, watching a DART go past. Geraldine took my hand.

'Why did you text me to ask about the word Concord?' she said. 'I'm surprised Shane even remembers it.'

'It was the old man who told me to ask you what the word meant.'

Geraldine withdrew her hand. 'Don't lie to me, Joey; don't you start playing mind games too.'

'Why would I lie?' I produced the scrap of paper. 'He wouldn't even say the word, he wrote it down.'

Geraldine examined the handwriting. 'You're certain you saw the old man write this?'

'Yes.'

She looked up. Her eyes seemed scared and unnaturally large. 'This is the same copperplate handwriting as the poem.'

'What does the word mean?'

'Concord is the brand of my mother's old wristwatch, my most precious possession. Two summers ago, Shane and I formed a private club. We swore to never say our password aloud to another living soul.'

'What was the password?'

Geraldine didn't reply, but I already knew the answer by her scared expression as she backed away from me. She turned and ran.

THIRTY-EIGHT

Thomas

December 2006

The well-dressed man seated beside Thomas in the New Jersey asylum stares at the doctor, who shrugs.

'Confessing to murder is a new ploy,' the doctor says, 'but Thomas would confess to anything simply to stay warm for the winter. He's turned up in every hospital I ever worked in and his madness always disappears on the first day of spring.' He smiles at Thomas. 'You needn't invent crimes, Thomas; no one is trying to throw you out into the snow. Besides, Mr Weinberg here is no policeman.'

Thomas scrutinises the stranger suspiciously as he leans forward.

'I'm an attorney-at-law, Mr McCormack. My company has our European headquarters in Dublin. I was visiting Ireland when your brother died, and I accompanied your brother's solicitor on his inventory of your childhood home.'

Thomas sits upright. 'Is that house still standing?'

Mr Weinberg nods. 'I'm not a superstitious man, Mr McCormack, but I've had the strangest dreams since returning to the States. That house packs quite an atmosphere.' He turns to the doctor. 'After they buried their mother, Mr McCormack's brothers stopped talking to each other. Neither ever married. Nobody else set foot inside the house. Pete lived upstairs and Frank downstairs. Locals called him Shotgun Frank because he would produce a shotgun if developers stood up on the wall to examine the site.'

The attorney turns to Thomas. 'Your brother Pete went slightly demented in old age. He grew a ponytail and claimed to hear voices. He was a familiar sight around Blackrock. When local people hadn't seen him for several weeks, Frank reluctantly allowed the police into the house, complaining that Pete was too lazy to get out of bed. Pete was dead in a bedroom filled with buzzing flies. The social workers could do little for Frank. He had gone daft with old age. A few months after Pete died, Frank was found dead, sitting out in the back garden holding a shotgun. Locals say he was obsessed with warding off a stray black cat that kept climbing up onto the wall.' Mr Weinberg sympathetically touches Thomas's shoulder. 'I'm sorry to bring bad tidings, Mr McCormack, but I have good news too.'

'What good news?'

'That house is worth a fortune as development land. Frank left it to you. For three years it has been rotting away in a legal limbo. That is, until I found you today.'

Thomas stares out the window. For seven decades he has tried to cover his tracks, but the whisperers had always gloated that, when the time came, he would be found. He can barely hear the attorney speaking because the voices keep whispering excitedly, We're going home.

'My wife claims you've become my obsession, Mr Mc-Cormack; you even crop up in my dreams. I never had to search harder to find anyone. It's like you tried to vanish from history.'

Thomas turns. 'What do you know about my history?'

'Reports trickled back to Ireland. Your brothers heard that when you were in the navy, you were the sole survivor when a ship sank. Eighteen days alone on a life raft. I checked your navy records. You were raving by the time you were found. They placed you in an asylum where you had everyone convinced you were a priest. Doctors located your family by asking Irish seminaries if they'd ever had a student of your name. Then, one morning, you discharged yourself and vanished again.'

'You had no right to find me,' Thomas says with sudden anger. 'I'm a patient in this asylum.'

'You've been a patient in many asylums and in several prisons. A nun noticed how you never had visitors. She traced your brothers and wrote to them, asking them to write to you.'

'I never liked nuns,' Thomas says. 'Sharp tongues, if you work for them.'

'The nun's letter caused your brothers to fall out,' Mr Weinberg continues. 'One wanted to write; the other said that you had broken your mother's heart. The doctor says you're the sanest man in this asylum, Mr McCormack.

You're also the richest. When you sell your house, you can buy the best medical care to make your remaining days as comfortable as possible.'

'Can I go home?' Thomas asks.

'I can arrange a flight. Indeed, I can even book you into the Blackrock Clinic next door to your old home.'

Thomas closes his eyes. The attorney wonders if he has fallen asleep. But he is reliving a memory of running down the Rock Road as a boy, chasing after a small aeroplane, punch-drunk with the possibilities of life ahead. He opens his eyes and looks at the attorney. 'I never expected them to choose a servant like you.'

'Who are they, Mr McCormack?'

'I will enter no clinic. That house may be sold only after I die. Next summer I will fly home to live in it.'

'Your cancer is well advanced,' the doctor says. 'You may not be alive then, Thomas.'

'Believe me, they won't let me die till I reach Blackrock.'

'I warn you, Mr McCormack,' the attorney says, 'it would take teams of workmen to make that house habitable.'

Thomas glares at the attorney. 'I don't want another soul to set foot inside it.'

'You will not find it a comfortable place to live.'

Thomas laughs, with a glint of triumph. 'I'm not going there to live, Mr Weinberg. I've something far more important to do there.'

THIRTY-NINE

Joey

November 2009

I didn't go straight home after Geraldine left me. I needed to try and make sense of things. I walked out to Booterstown Marsh and climbed over the fence to sit in that wilderness of wild birds, watching the trains go past. It was seven o'clock when I reached Brusna Cottages and opened the front door. Immediately I knew something was wrong. Normally Mum had the radio on for company, but there was a worrying silence and a smell I never associated with my home: the stench of alcohol. Then I heard a faint sobbing from the living room.

I stood in the hallway, scared of what I might see when I opened the door. Mum sat with her back to me. At her feet lay three red roses, an upturned glass and a half-empty vodka bottle. I knew by the strong smell that a large amount of vodka had seeped into the carpet. Mum was crying. I didn't know what I should do, so I sat on the edge of her chair and put my arms softly around her shoulders. I thought she would turn and embrace me, but instead she flinched at my touch. She stood up.

'I don't understand why you would do this to me, Joey.'

'What do you mean, Mum?'

'Is this your idea of a joke? Are you trying to be clever or to taunt me?'

'Mum, what's wrong?'

She turned with a bewildered look. 'It was the maddest thing, Joey. When I walked in and saw the three red roses, for half a second I thought your father's ghost had been here.'

'Have you been drinking?'

Her eyes grew colder. 'Is that what this is about? What you wanted to achieve? Did you want to find me drunk, slurring my words, back on the booze after fifteen years of fighting against temptation? I rarely go out because I can't bear being in pubs or near alcohol. Just because I stopped drinking doesn't mean I stopped being an alcoholic, Joey. I'm what they call a dry drunk. After your dad died I wanted to drink myself to death. But I couldn't, because I had you to mind. I had never even tasted alcohol until your dad bought me vodka on our first date. When you're shy, life seems easier after a few drinks. When we first kissed, his lips tasted of alcohol. After he died, every sip of vodka reminded me of him. I never talk much about him, but I'll tell you one thing – he never possessed an ounce of malice. He would never have done what you did to me this evening.'

'Mum, I've done nothing to you.'

Mum picked up the bottle and walked into the kitchen. She poured the remaining vodka down the sink and hurled the empty bottle into the bin. She stood at the window with her back to me.

'Don't lie to me, Joey. It's like you were toying with me, deliberately trying to find my breaking point. Have I passed your test, Joey, or what other temptations do you feel you need to put in front of me? If you wanted to break my will then you almost got your wish because when I walked in here and heard your dad's voice, I longed to start drinking again and to never stop.'

'How could you hear his voice? Mum, I don't know what you're talking about.'

'I'm talking about coming home from work, exhausted, to find your dad's demo tape playing in the living room at full blast. You left it on, knowing that I didn't want to ever hear his voice again. And then you opened a bottle of vodka and poured me the first glass in advance. You even poured half the bottle all over the carpet so that the whole place would stink of drink. Then, like a final taunt, you arranged three roses on the floor like your dad promised to do in the first song on the tape – the first song he ever wrote for me.'

'Mum, you know I wouldn't do any of this.'

'Do I? I thought I knew your father, but there were things I only discovered about him after we married. Those songs brought all those things back, Joey. I turned the tape off but I've been sitting here for the past hour, shaking with such longing for a drink that my knuckles turned white.'

'Tell me you didn't take a drink, Mum.'

'Fifteen years ago, when I threw away every reminder of that gutless husband of mine, I swore to never drink again. I've kept my promise, something he wasn't espe-cially good at.'

'Please don't call Dad gutless,' I pleaded. 'I never heard you say a bad word about him before.'

'Maybe it's time to be honest. He was too gutless to ever make a record. He said he was chasing immortality, but I know he was just too scared of failure.'

She turned around. I could see the hurt and confusion within her.

'I swear to you, Mum, I never even got the demo tape off Mr Quinn.'

'Are you saying it walked here all by itself, stopping to buy vodka on the way? It let itself in with its own key at the exact time I was coming home from work?'

Suddenly I realised who the culprit was. But there was no sign of a break-in. Then I remembered the night when I left my school bag at Shane's place before the mid-term history exam. He must have made a copy of the key I kept in it before giving it back.

'It wasn't me,' I said.

'Then who would do such a thing?'

Somebody who wished to drive a wedge between my mum and me. Shane's own words came back, 'Never be-friend a loner.' Behind all his charm, Shane was a loner. The people in our class might think they knew him. But they only saw the masks he used to hide his loneliness.

'Shane did this.'

'Why?'

'Because he's jealous I have someone who loves me.'

'Why should I believe you?'

'Because I'm your son.'

'I believed a man because he was my husband. But he made a fool of me.'

'Stop saying that, Mum.' Her words were stripping away the myths from my father. 'You make it sound like you hated him.'

'I loved him; that's why his betrayals still hurt,' Mum said, 'why I've never been able to talk about them. I could live with us barely having food on the table. I was happy to work every hour to give him the space to be a genius. But I only started drinking heavily to ease the pain of finding that I was playing second fiddle to every young blonde who made eyes at him. If your dad had lived, Joey, we would have separated. You would only see him every Sunday when he took you to McDonald's or the zoo.'

'If he remembered to turn up,' I said, shocked to feel bitter towards a figure I had always idolised. Mum's anger turned to concern.

'For you, he would have always turned up, Joey. The minute you were born, I saw an unbreakable bond between you. It made me jealous. He might have let me down, but he'd have walked barefoot through the gates of hell if you ever needed him.'

'Please say that you believe I didn't put that tape on to torment you.'

'I don't know what to believe,' she said.

'I swear I would never lie to you. I'm not like Dad was.' The words felt like a betrayal. Was this what Shane wanted:

not only to drive a wedge between Mum and me, but to destroy the grip that my dad had on my imagination?

'I do believe you,' she said, sensing what price those words cost me. 'But why would your friend do this?'

'That's what I'm going to find out.'

Mum tried to wrap her arms around me, but I was too angry to be stopped. My only thought was to find Shane. Mum called after me, begging me to come back, but I was beyond listening. My knuckles were clenched, and as I strode onto Main Street, only a fool would have got in my way.

FORTY

Joey

November 2009

At half past eight, I reached Shane's place on Pine Lawn. I knocked so aggressively that Mrs Higgins opened the door at once, alarmed at my agitated state.

'Where is he?'

Shane's door opened. From the way he stood I knew that he had been expecting me. Mrs Higgins glanced at us both.

'There's no trouble, boys, is there?'

'Why would there be trouble, Mrs Higgins?' Shane asked.

'You both just look …'

'I promised to help Joey with his history homework. Come in, Joey.' Shane beckoned. 'We won't disturb you, Mrs Higgins.'

I entered his room. He closed the door. We listened to the woman's footsteps retreating down the hallway. Once her kitchen door closed, I grabbed Shane, thrusting him against the door.

'I'll kill you for what you've done!'

'Calm down, Joey.' Shane seemed more amused than

alarmed. 'You won't kill anyone. Sit down and tell me what you're talking about.'

'I'm talking about you trying to come between me and my mum.'

'Why would I want to do that?'

'You broke into my house.'

'Well, you broke into mine.'

I released my grip and stepped back. 'What did you say?'

'Last night. I told you to ignore that old man, but you're weak, like your dad was. Temptation and curiosity were always going to get the better of you.'

I grabbed his shirt again. 'Mention my dad again and I'll burst you.'

Shane gripped my wrists and prised away my grip, making a whispering noise as if calming a frightened animal. 'Did you think I wouldn't know you visited that house last night?'

'You're not natural,' I said. 'You know too much about everything. I never even told you my mum had a drink problem.'

'You didn't have to.' He relaxed his grip. 'Their life story is written in your dad's lyrics, a golden courtship halted by the advent of a baby. Three red roses indeed. You know something, Joey? I think you were an unplanned surprise. You put an end to the roses. Maybe his death was for the best. It prevented your mum from becoming a drunken lush, trailing around behind him from one failed dream to the next.'

I punched Shane so hard that blood spouted from his nose. His head smashed back against the door. I thought he would retaliate, but he just grimaced and walked past me to sit in the armchair.

'What stories did the old man spin for you last night?'

'He's demented,' I said, 'convinced that he's a teenager and you have stolen his body.'

'He sounds demented. I mean, who would believe such a crazy story?' Shane laughed but he was watching my reaction with deadly seriousness. 'Would you?'

'What do you mean?'

'Only that it would be the ultimate theft – to steal someone else's identity. They used to have a name for such people: changelings. It's all superstition, of course. But just suppose that when people die they don't go away. What if, every time you walk along a street, you are brushing through clouds of swirling ghosts, but you're too busy with your trivial concerns to hear their pleas? What if there always needed to be one person alive who can hear their whispers and so keep them alive too?'

'You sound like Thomas.'

Shane walked over to the sink. He wetted a towel and washed the blood off his face. 'Maybe I am like him. Maybe each time I stare into this mirror I see his face and a line of other faces. Did you ever think that just maybe he might be telling the truth?'

'You're as daft as each other.' My anger was turning to unease.

'And as lonely. I envy you for having your mother's

love, Joey, like I envy the fact that one day you will die.'

'We all die.'

'Do we?' Shane turned from the mirror and sat on the bed. 'Have you any idea how old I am, Joey? How lonely it is to always live my life alone?'

The front door opened and the students who lived upstairs passed within a few feet of us on the other side of Shane's closed bedroom door. I wanted to call out for help, but how could I tell anyone that I had a sense of a net closing in?

'What do you want from me?'

'I want to know again what it feels like to be normal,' Shane replied. 'To know what it feels like to experience things for the first time. I want to be at your side when life unfolds. I want you to kiss Geraldine for me because Geraldine will never kiss me. Even if she did, I could not truly taste her lips because mine are too parched with age. My taste buds are dry. I lack your special quality.'

'What quality?'

'Innocence. The magic of life lies ahead for you and you can make it real for me too by letting me share it. I feel stale because I have tasted everything before, but I cannot endure another lifetime on my own. I want you as my friend, Joey. We can travel the world together. I have enough money and cunning to make you famous. It's what your talent deserves – the immortality your father missed out on. I've lived dozens of lives already, yet it feels like I have never truly lived. But this time, you and I will share in every experience and you will make them all real for me.'

'You're insane,' I said.

Shane glanced towards the door. 'And you will go insane too if you walk away from my offer; you'll go crazy with curiosity. I'm offering you fame, Joey, because I can make it happen. Don't say you're not tempted: temptation runs in your family. Did you find your mother drunk on the floor?'

'She poured the vodka down the sink.'

'Another reason for you to leave her – you're not like her; you're more like your dad. Once your dad saw a temptation he simply had to taste it. It's time you tasted fame, Joey. Fame will be the greatest party this side of the Hellfire Club. Walk away from me and you'll be leaving behind the best friend you'll ever have.'

I stood up to leave. 'Whoever you are, you're no friend of mine.'

'A true friend will do anything for you. Look.' Shane reached under his bed to produce an old spool of recording tape. 'Bongo Drums has a huge attic. Do you know how many boxes I needed to break open to find the right tape? I had to ransack his house then, because if this tape alone was missing, you'd be a suspect. When he arrived home unexpectedly, I even had to put on a mask and smash in his face, just to protect you.'

'It has nothing to do with me.'

'Did you hear the tape?'

'No.'

'Then listen. Every day I hear dozens of dead voices. It's time you had the guts to hear the voice you're so scared of.'

'Go to hell,' I hissed. But I was too mesmerised to

leave as Shane threaded the spools onto an old-fashioned tape recorder.

'I am in hell,' Shane replied, calmly. 'Blackrock is my private hell. I could not escape this place, even when I travelled the world. I've been a mute pig-killer, a murderer, a rake, a sea captain, a monk, a serving boy. I seduced a young Fleming girl in a field of wheat, and several life-times later saw her great-granddaughter break into my lair as a doe-eyed, scared child.'

With a soft click, the tape finished rewinding. Shane held his finger over the play button.

'You look angry and scared, Joey. I wish I could feel those emotions. I'd give twenty years of my life to be you for a day. But that's easy to say when I can't seem to let myself die. I possess immortality. It's what your father always wanted.'

I wanted to walk out into the night air. I opened the door into Mrs Higgins's hallway and took a few steps away from Shane's room. But I could go no further, because I was mesmerised by the voice coming from the tape recorder: a voice both familiar and strange. The voice told Ben Quinn and the other backing musicians to take it from the top, then started to sing. Bittersweet, tender and breathtaking, my father's lyrics lured me back into Shane's lair. He sat beside the tape recorder, listening intently.

'I can hear you in him,' he said. 'You're his son in every respect.'

'At least I know who I am.'

Shane nodded. 'You're a good person, whereas I'm

neither bad nor good. But I have learned how to plot and scheme and think five moves ahead. Singers like you are always undone by inexperience. You get so wrapped up in your songs that you make poor business decisions. You deserve to play stadiums but wind up playing shabby hotel lounges. That won't happen if you let me guide you. I can make you more famous – than you could ever wish for. You won't even have to sell your soul. All I ask is that you become my friend.'

'Go to hell,' I said again, more weakly this time.

'There are worse places than hell, Joey: there's limbo. That's where your father is. Listen to his lyrics. You can make him famous: these songs are your inheritance. I can get you any record deal you want, any drug or any woman. I can make people do things without them realising I'm pulling the strings. Just share fully in my life and let me fully share yours. I've brought your father back from the dead. He's standing behind you, ashamed of how he wasted this talent. Give him this second chance. Think of the lyrics you'll write when I can tell you the words he's whispering in your ear.'

I was only half-listening because I had turned to stare at the empty space where Shane claimed my father stood. I felt a rage within me.

'Leave my life alone.'

'Joey, I know your every thought. I've seen your type so often.'

'Turn off that tape.'

'It's too late, Joey; you've heard his voice. His voice will never leave your head, just like I will never leave your side.'

Shane stopped talking then. He stared over my shoulder, suddenly terrified. It was as if he had been bluffing, but was now confronted by a genuine presence. I felt the room turn ice-cold. I could see nothing, but I heard a voice in my head – the same voice I had heard that night on Bull Island. The voice whispered one word: 'Run'.

FORTY-ONE

Joey

November 2009

After I left Shane's house I didn't know where to go. I could not tell Mum about this because she would think I was insane. Music blared from a house further down Pine Lawn. In the front room, teenage girls in short dresses shrieked with laughter as they dolled themselves up before heading out for the Wes disco in Donnybrook. A ruck of lads tossed a rugby ball around the driveway as they waited for their dates to come out. Two teenagers were emerging from the park that stretched around the back of Newtownpark House to the homes on Mount Albany. One flashed a bottle of vodka from inside his jacket, provoking a cheer from his peers in the driveway to acknowledge his success at having procured it. His companion was cradling two six-packs of cans in his arms. They were walking straight into my path but I was in no mood to change direction. With their friends watching, neither were they. However, they parted slightly just before I barged through them.

'You watch yourself, pal,' the guy with the vodka said. I turned. 'Why? What are you going to do about it?'

For sixteen years, I had been a blank canvas, willing to be shaped by other people's expectations. I had never raised a fist to anyone, but I was full of rage now, so confused by Shane's mind games, and so angry at his invasion of my mum's privacy, that I was spoiling for a fight. I would have happily taken on all the boys in the driveway, even if they beat me into a pulp. I would have kept getting back up, because being punched seemed preferable to trying to work out the impossible thoughts in my head. I reached inside the guy's jacket and removed his bottle of vodka.

'Screw you,' I said and walked past him into the park. I expected them to attack me under the old trees, but something in my stride made them hesitate, as if awed by my audacity. Then amid their angry shouts I heard a familiar voice and knew that Shane had emerged from his house to quieten them in that soft tone he used. I knew that he would give them the price of a replacement bottle and then follow me across that park because his loneliness would not allow him to let me go. In his room I had been seduced by his lies, but now, out in the night air as I passed evening figures playing tennis in the courts, I dismissed him and Thomas as fantasists. What I could not dismiss was the palpable sense that my father's ghost had been present in Shane's room.

I opened the bottle and took my first gulp. The raw taste of the vodka made me want to throw up. My throat was on fire, my eyes temporarily blinded. But I took a second slug and then a third even deeper one as I crossed the grass towards the lights of the houses on Mount Albany. I didn't look back, but I knew that Shane was following. I felt rage at everything he had done. I also felt nauseated and light-headed from the vodka. I wanted to stop drinking and yet I wanted to finish the bottle. Thankfully, I didn't finish it, but half the bottle was gone before I hurled it into a driveway, enjoying the reckless sound of glass smashing. I was unsteady and yet pumped full of energy. Shane was not going to manipulate my life any longer. I would show him that I could take any risk he took. A car was double parked outside a house on Mount Albany, the engine running as a young Chinese man delivered pizza. The girl paying him in her doorway was rooting for change. I stopped beside the empty car with its door ajar and heard Shane's hurried footsteps approach.

'What are you thinking of doing?' Shane hissed.

'Maybe I'll bring you to a gig in style, for a change.'

'You can't drive.'

'It's an automatic. How hard can it be?'

Pretty hard, as I discovered after I sat into the driver's seat. The pizza man was still preoccupied with counting change. Shane opened the passenger door and hissed, 'Are you crazy?'

Maybe I was. When Shane saw me release the hand brake he jumped in. The car shot forward. I needed to brake fiercely to prevent us colliding with a parked vehicle.

'For God's sake, at least let me drive,' Shane snapped.

I ignored him as the car shot forward again. I was in the middle of the road, trying to get to grips with the steering wheel. I heard a shout and, in the rear-view mirror, saw the delivery man chase after us. The car veered from side to side, narrowly missing parked vehicles. Shane was screaming at me to stop. He wanted to grab the steering wheel but was too scared in case the car spun out of control. This lack of control scared him, I realised: the fact that he was no longer the one in charge of the game. From the moment we met, I had let him control our friendship. But this time he would go where I decided. He had messed with my head, but now I would mess with his. I felt a sense of power as the car surged forward, a sense of finally being his equal.

'To the Eagle Tavern,' I shouted, repeating a phrase he sometimes used.

My drunken euphoria and the sense of control only lasted until we reached the top of the cul-de-sac where a pedestrian entrance led into the Springhill Park estate. Somehow I managed to turn the car, which veered onto the footpath, narrowly avoiding a wall. I manoeuvred us back onto the roadway, but we skidded and banged against a parked SUV, setting off its alarm. I straightened up so we were heading back towards the angry delivery man who tried to block the road but then jumped from our path.

'You've gone crazy,' Shane hissed as I reached the junction with Newtownpark Avenue. 'This isn't like you at all.'

'How do you know what I'm like?' I swung right, narrowly missing cars coming from both directions. 'Maybe I have a mind of my own.'

'Then use it. Stop this car before we're both killed.'

I saw genuine fear in his eyes. 'You can't die.' I taunted him. 'How could a car accident kill an immortal being?'

'Don't get smart,' Shane snapped, 'it doesn't suit you.'

'You're a fantasist, a spoof.'

'You don't know what you're talking about.'

'I know you and Thomas are equally crazy.'

Shane gripped my elbow. 'Brake!'

We had sped past the garage and the church and were approaching the traffic lights at the junction with Stradbook Road. I had to swerve into the other lane because I could not stop in time. Cars approaching us swung up onto the footpath. Somehow, I managed to turn left without hitting anyone and we found ourselves speeding down Temple Hill.

'How did your aunt in England really die?' I said.

'She crashed her car because she couldn't cope with living with me. The more I tried to befriend her, the more scared she became.' He flinched as car horns beeped in protest because I was unable to stay in one lane. 'Where are we going?'

'There's an old dairy I'd like you to visit.'

Terror entered Shane's eyes. 'That old man is using you.'

'No one is using me. I want the truth for once.'

'You'll need to kill me before I'd set foot back in that house.'

Shane had the passenger door open. He was going to jump and risk being killed rather than be brought any closer to Castledawson Avenue.

'Stop!' I shouted.

He looked back. 'You think you're in charge, but someone else is always pulling the strings.'

I hit the brake as he swung his feet out the open door.
The car began to skid. The rage that had possessed me
was gone. I just knew at that moment that I would do anything not to die. Yet I could not control whether I did or
not. The car spun like a die, its back wheels mounting the
kerb. It almost overturned. Then it stopped with a final
crash against the side of a deserted bus shelter. The adver-
tisement on the bus shelter exploded, shards of glass
drumming down on the roof of the car.

FORTY-TWO

Joey

November 2009

I found I couldn't move. There seemed to be no strength left in my body. It was a miracle that the bus stop was deserted and we had killed nobody. I had just committed the most irresponsible act of my life, and I felt so shocked that I didn't care what happened to me. I would have sat there until the police came, but Shane got out and pulled open my door. He hauled me from the car.

'Head case,' he said, 'You're a head case. Now run.'

Still I couldn't move. Then I heard sirens and an instinct for self-preservation took over. Suddenly I was running, even though furious drivers who had stopped their cars were trying to block my path. But nobody was going to catch me as I dodged them and raced into St Vincent's Park. No matter how fast I ran, however, I could hear Shane's footsteps behind me. When we were safely out of sight of Temple Hill, he lunged forward and rugby tackled me. I fell onto the roadway, with Shane on top of me, his knees pinning my arms, his fists aiming blows at my face.

'You bloody fool,' he said. 'All I wanted was a friend.

Maybe I invent things, but so would you if you saw your parents die in a house fire.'

Shane stopped hitting me and sat hunched beside me on the ground while I looked up through the film of blood from my busted nose.

'My fists hurt,' Shane said quietly.

'My face hurts more.'

'On our first day in school you were scared of your own shadow. I may have spun you a few lies, but I brought you out of your shell.'

I rose and wiped the blood off my face. My knees were badly grazed. I looked down at Shane. I wanted to walk away and never see him again.

'I don't believe a word from your mouth anymore,' I said quietly.

Shane looked up as if sizing me up and coming to a decision. 'Do you want the truth?'

'Yes. What age are you for a start?'

He gestured as if this was the dumbest question he had ever heard. 'Use your eyes, Joey. I'm sixteen. I'm a messer who likes to stir things up. I fed you the same lies that I knew the old man would feed you. He is crazy and probably actually believes he is me. But I was just messing with your head, winding you up for fun.'

'Then why were you so terrified of me bringing you to his house?'

Shane looked pathetic, hunched on the tarmac. I was keeping one eye out for any sign of the police. 'His house gives me the creeps; too many bad memories.' He looked up. 'I'm utterly alone in life, Joey, and when you're lonely, you make things up. I'm trying to be good here, so stay away from me, you hear? But stay away from Thomas too. Don't let him use you, Joey. He wants Geraldine. It's grotesque, but he secretly fancies her. I wouldn't trust him alone with her. I wouldn't trust him alone with anyone.'

I walked away and left Shane sitting on the footpath. I felt sick from the vodka and the blows to my face, and deeply ashamed for having stolen that car. I desperately needed somebody to put their arms around me. I walked until I reached Geraldine's house. I knew there was blood on my face. But, having cleaned myself up as best I could, I knocked. Her gran opened the front door quickly – far too quickly.

'You're Joey.' She eyed me carefully.

'Is Geraldine in?'

'What's after happening to you? Have you been drinking? Where's my granddaughter?' The woman peered anxiously down the path.

'Why would I know where she is?'

'Because she ran out the door at seven o'clock and I never saw her look so tense. She wouldn't say where she was going, but I sensed she was going to meet a young man. Was she going to break it off with you?'

'We're not even going out,' I said.

'She talks about you often enough, she's more than fond of you.' The woman stopped. 'Where is she? She was in such an agitated state and she's been gone for hours. Think, Joey. Is there anyone else she might have gone to see?'

Shane's words came back: he secretly fancies her. This afternoon I had fed her the mad fantasy which the old man had concocted, the notion that the boy she once loved was trapped inside his ancient body. Thomas had used me to lure her to his house. I couldn't explain this to her gran. I simply turned and ran towards Castledawson Avenue.

FORTY-THREE

Joey

November 2009

When I reached Castledawson Avenue I scrambled over the tumbledown wall and landed in the tangle of sky-high nettles in the garden. I didn't care how often I got stung; I needed to reach that house before anything happened to Geraldine. Maybe I was too late, and it would be my turn to find two bodies there. The back door was wide open, as if somebody had rushed in. The kitchen was unearthly quiet. Finding my way by whatever moonlight came through the grime-coated windows, I reached the back stairs with every nerve end in my body screaming at me to leave.

There was something unnatural about the weight of the silence surrounding me. I mistrusted it, sensing that it was not silence at all, but a babble of voices, if I could only hear them. Spectres trying to grab at my hair, screaming with rage, resenting my intrusion. I turned around and sensed that they had stopped too. They were not holding their breath because they had long since ceased to breathe. But they were watching, willing me to flee back out into the night air.

I felt scared without knowing what I was scared of.

Two months ago I would not have allowed myself to be here. Back then, I had wanted to keep my head down. But Shane was right; his friendship had shaken up my life. I could almost visualise two versions of myself at war on that dark stairway. Behind me in the kitchen was the timid, bullied boy that I had been. He was begging me to leave. Ahead of me, scared but determined to continue, was the young man that I wanted to become: neither Shane's sidekick nor a mirror image of my father, but an independent person who made decisions for himself. If there was a chance that Geraldine might be in this house, then, no matter what, I was determined to bring her out.

I entered the hallway, my eyes growing accustomed to the dark, my ears alert for any sound. I no longer felt surrounded by unseen presences. I felt utterly alone. If anything happened to me, I might never be found here. But what could happen? I was young and strong. Thomas was a feeble man whom I could easily overpower. Then I heard a sound as faint as a sigh or a drip of water. But I knew it was a human voice. I crossed the empty hallway and spied a glimmer of candlelight through the living-room doorway.

If Thomas was holding Geraldine imprisoned in there, I would kill him. If he had touched one hair on her head, I would tear his limbs apart. Softly, I pushed open the door. The old man sat in an ancient armchair, with Geraldine kneeling beside him, her hand reaching up to stroke his lined face. Both of them seemed to be in tears. Geraldine gave no impression of being trapped or coerced.

They looked like lovebirds who had found each other again after a long separation. It was a sickening image, and all the more disturbing because Geraldine looked so wide-eyed and lost, like a character in a David Lynch film. I slammed my fist against the door. The sound must have startled them, because they both glanced in my direction.

'What are you doing here, Joey?' Geraldine's voice sounded distracted, as if she was in deep shock, like she felt trapped inside a nightmare.

I stepped forward. 'Come on, Geraldine, let's go.'

The old man placed his hand possessively on Geraldine's shoulder. 'You brought her to me as I knew you would, Joey, and I thank you for that. Now stop trespassing in my house. This is none of your concern.'

'You used me to lure her here. Take your hands off her.'

'Go away, Joey,' Geraldine said and her voice sounded as if she was hypnotised. 'Can't you see that I am free to choose where I want to be? I could never fully love you, because I loved somebody else – someone I thought I had lost. I didn't understand this before tonight, because this is the first time I've been alone with Shane since the night the police found two bodies unconscious downstairs in this house. You can't recognise the truth because you never knew the real Shane. But I loved him and he is not the person standing behind you.'

I turned to see Shane in the doorway. He was shivering, his eyes scared.

'Where did you come from?' I asked.

The old man tried to rise, but Geraldine forced him back into his chair. Shane shook his head sadly.

'I warned you to keep Geraldine safe from him, Joey. Now look at what you've done. He's like a spider weaving his web around a fly. I dread this house, but I followed you because I couldn't see you enter here alone, and I couldn't see Geraldine get hurt.'

'Shane won't hurt me,' Geraldine said quietly.

'I am Shane,' the young figure in the doorway said.

'You're not.'

He brushed past me and entered the room. 'Trust me, Geraldine; I am. Can't you see that we both are: that we are two sides of the one coin? The Shane you once loved still exists as much inside of me as inside the old sack of bones in that armchair.'

'You're spinning lies again,' I snapped. 'Half an hour ago you told me this nonsense was make-believe.'

'I told you what you needed to hear, Joey, after I re-alised that you could never accept the truth. I should not have tried to recruit you as a friend, but I got lonely. Anyone who has lived as often as I have would get lonely at the prospect of another lifetime on my own. But you cannot give me companionship – no mortal being can. So leave this house, and take Geraldine with you. I have put off this confrontation for too long. This is between me and him, and nobody else.'

'Between you and who?' I asked.

'Me and my blood brother here, my other half.' He laughed. 'We're related through bad blood that stretches back to when nothing existed around here except an out-crop of black rock marking the boundaries of Dublin. Back to when the first practitioner of this dark art learned how to cheat death by stashing his soul inside the body of each new victim, like a set of matryoshka dolls. I cannot tell you who I am, Joey, because I am no one person. I am sixteen and I am six hundred years of age. I am the carrier of a disease called immortality. That haggard old body shouldn't still be here, but for two years I've been too weak to kill him. I have avoided this house, because I did not want to add another murder to the sins on my conscience.'

'Conscience?' The elderly figure snorted with disgust. 'Where was your conscience when you let my father die in that house fire?'

'It was regrettable, but necessary. Now, you wanted a fight to the death and here I am. When we are finished there will be no more confusion over who is who any more. It's time you joined me in this new body; it is time that we were one.'

Geraldine stood in front of the old man.

'I won't let you touch him,' she said.

The old man rose and shoved Geraldine to one side. She fell, and landed awkwardly, twisting her ankle as she slipped on the debris on the floor. He ignored her cry of pain as he produced a black-handled knife from his over-coat. 'I knew I could lure you back here with the right bait,' he taunted. 'You always had a thing for Geraldine. "Step into my parlour, said the spider to the fly." Your words on the night Geraldine and I broke in. Well, this time I'm the spider and you're the fly. You stole my youth, you soul-snatcher, and now I want it back.'

'There is only one way I can give it back.' The younger figure circled cagily, beyond range of the knife. 'You know this, because our minds are like one; we hear the same voices. But I gave you something the voices never meant you to have: continued life. I refused to do their bidding because your grandfather and I were friends once. I made the mistake of letting you live on inside my old body.'

Geraldine grimaced as she struggled to rise: but she couldn't put any weight on her busted ankle that was already starting to swell. She begged me to separate them as the older figure sliced through the air with his knife.

'This is not living,' he shouted. 'Two years ago I was a boy. Now look at me, trapped like this.' He swung the blade again, summoning what little strength he possessed. 'Why could you not have ended the curse by dying here alone?'

The teenage figure nimbly dodged the blade. 'And why did you have to break in?' he replied. 'I bolted the front door and lived by the flames of two candles. Yet still your curiosity made you seek me out, your greed for money, a greed they could exploit.'

The older figure almost fell as he swung the knife again. The boy gripped his hand to steady him, making no attempt to confiscate the blade.

'Seventy years ago, I made a wish to see the world. The voices granted me my wish a thousand times over. I knelt to bless hobos who fell from freight trains. I trawled for lost souls like a beachcomber trawls for driftwood. I fooled myself into believing I was doing God's work, but I was not saving souls; I was keeping them trapped inside me, like bees buzzing in a jar.'

'Then lift up your T-shirt,' the old figure pleaded. 'I will gladly cut out your heart and set them all free.'

'If you stab this young body then you will kill us both and you're not ready to die either. I admit that I stole your body. Now there is only one way to get it back. I know you're frightened because I was frightened too when I found myself, as a fourteen-year-old boy, forced to live inside the body of a mute hunchback. It took four years for me to found the courage to liberate myself by allowing that changeling, that usurper, to slit the throat of the ancient body I was trapped inside. I remember the searing pain of the blade, but the pain gave way to liberation, and when I opened my eyes again I was staring out through my old eyes once more, and that mute had become merely another ghost living on inside me. Let me cut the throat of my old body, Shane: let me cut you free to inhabit your own body again.'

'I want it back; I want my life back.' The old figure lunged forward angrily. The younger figure circled, keeping beyond the reach of the blade.

'Then lower the knife. There is no other way. Soon we will only possess one body between us. Thomas McCormack will be just one more voice in your head. Give me the knife.'

'Who … are … you?' Geraldine's scared voice was barely above a whisper. The young figure glanced at her.

'I am Thomas McCormack, a spoiled priest. I am Joseph Nally, a mute dogsbody for the nuns. I am Michael Byrne, the upstart gambler who built this house. I am Henry Dawson, the consumptive rake who gambled away Castledawson House. I am names vanished from history. I am a hive of jostling souls whose secrets are known only to me.'

As the voices inside the teenage body spoke, the old figure lunged forward with the knife and missed. The boy waited until he regained his footing, then calmly stepped forward to within range of the blade. He stripped off his Pixies T-shirt. Beads of sweat glistened on his naked chest.

'If you wish for us both to die, then I will make it easy for you,' he said quietly. 'I will even point the blade for you. Just remember that it is pointed at your own heart. If you kill me, you will kill yourself, because the body you occupy is too old to live on for much longer. But if I cut your throat, we shall become one. We can dominate the other voices in this chain and, when the time comes, we can find the strength to end this curse together. You want to live, Shane; I know this, because I know every secret in your soul.'

'What about this pair?' The old figure glanced at Geraldine and me. 'How do they fit into your plan?'

'I haven't decided yet,' the teenager replied. 'It is my own fault for making the mistake of wanting to have a friend.'

The elderly figure lowered the knife wearily. 'You have

everything worked out. You're such a convincing liar that the police will believe you broke in here and found all three of us dead. They will believe that a deluded old man knifed Geraldine and was disturbed by Joey. They will conclude that Joey and the old man stabbed each other to death in a tussle. Not only did you want a friend this time, you even schemed to make Geraldine your lover. But intimacy is too dangerous for the souls inside you. So you'll add more corpses to all those who have impeded your path to immortality. I thought I had lured you here tonight, but you lured us all here. You had not finalised your plans until now, but the evil voices are taking you over. I know your plan. Your plan is to kill us all.'

FORTY-FOUR

Joey

November 2009

Holding the knife by the blade, the old man offered the hilt to Shane. 'Kill me first, so,' he whispered. 'Then, together, we can deal with the others.'

I felt paralysed with fear, but Geraldine managed to rise to her feet. As the boy reached for the knife she hurled a cup at him. Instinctively, he ducked. As he did so, the elderly figure flicked the knife around and rammed the blade savagely into the boy's stomach. The boy doubled up in agony, but he was not alone in this pain. The old figure dropped the black-handled knife and grasped his own stomach, as if he too had been stabbed. Both sank to their knees, doubled up in a mirror image of each other.

Geraldine tried to hobble past them, but the boy grabbed a handful of her hair. I punched him and he let go, sinking to his knees. He managed to grasp Geraldine's leg, but I kicked his fingers until he released his grip. Geraldine was free and we could make for the door. But with her ankle injured, our progress was nightmarishly slow. We reached the dark hallway and hobbled slowly towards the back stairs.

I heard footsteps behind us – slow and feeble, but gaining ground. I lifted Geraldine into my arms as we reached the narrow stairs. The passageway was pitch-dark, but I would have kept my footing if a bony hand had not pushed me down the last few steps. I fell forward and, as we landed, I heard the sickening thud of Geraldine's skull striking the flagstones. A stray black cat bolted from the shadows. The wrenching pain in my shoulder told me that I had dislocated it. A hand reached down to grab my jacket. It was the old man with the outward appearance of Thomas McCormack, but who claimed to be Shane O'Driscoll.

'Trust me,' he said. 'The changeling is bleeding heavily upstairs. He can't live much longer. Is she alive?'

'She's unconscious. I don't think it's safe to move her.'

'Then leave her here.'

'I'm not leaving her. My shoulder is in so much pain that I can't move anyway.'

'You're coming with me.'

He grabbed my jacket in both hands, and dragged me along the stone floor with fierce determination. I kept screaming because every jolt was torture. He hauled me down a narrow passageway where the walls seemed to close in. It felt like a nightmare, but nobody could have slept through the pain in my shoulder. The old man dragged me into a cellar and then collapsed, panting heavily. Maybe we were all doomed, Shane bleeding to death upstairs and Geraldine having suffered a broken neck. I gazed towards the sprawled figure on the flagstones.

'Don't you die on me,' I hissed, 'Don't you dare have a heart attack and leave me here.'

He fumbled in his clothes for a box of matches. I saw an outline of the low-roofed cellar before the first match went out. He struck a second match, and managed to light the stump of a candle. He melted some wax onto a flag-stone, then fixed the stump upright in the hot wax. The cen-tral flagstone was missing. A primeval instinct told me there was water there that I could drown in. I tried to rise, but could only crawl a few painful inches. We listened to foot-steps stumble down the sloping passageway towards us.

'Do you still have the knife?' I whispered.

The old man shook his head, as if the effort to speak was too much. Then the Shane I knew appeared, carrying Geraldine's limp body. He sank to his knees, laying her gently on the floor.

'Has anybody got something soft for her head?' he asked.

Geraldine's clothes were covered in blood from the wound on the boy's side. His stomach and jeans were soaked, and I knew that he must have left a trail of blood all the way from upstairs.

'You need to get to a doctor,' the old man whispered. 'You've lost too much blood. I can feel the life draining from me too.'

'It's too late,' the boy said. 'You're after killing us both, Shane.'

'I don't want to die, Thomas.' The older figure's voice grew faint. 'I thought I did, but I'm too scared.'

'I've faced death a dozen times,' the boy said. 'Each time, I swore to go through with it, but a drowning man will cling to anything to live on for even one extra second.'

Both went quiet and I became aware of them looking at me. They seemed to possess a single mind, understanding each other's thoughts.

'No,' I said. 'No, to whatever you are planning.'

Both edged closer. I tried to sit up but the pain in my shoulder was too great. I went to kick out, but the younger figure had anticipated this. He threw himself across my knees to pin me down. The old man's face pressed close to mine.

'Make a wish for us,' he coaxed. 'Make any wish you want: wish for fame as a musician, for immortality. It will be granted.'

'Go to hell.'

'Hell?' Both laughed bitterly, speaking simultaneously. 'We are already trapped in hell. If you want to understand the meaning of hell, look around you, Joey.'

'And you expect me to join you?' I hissed. 'You expect me to take my place in your line of trapped souls?'

'What choice have you?' they said. 'We're both going to die and you can barely move. Neither you nor Geraldine will find a way out. Nobody will think to look for you here. You will eventually die of thirst and starvation. But this does not have to be the end. The three of us can live on; we can all share your body. Just wish for something good. Geraldine is unconscious; her neck may be broken after that fall. Use your wish to get her safely away from here, because she is the one person that all three of us love.'

As they spoke, they were dragging me across the flag-stones until I lay face down, staring into the well. The younger figure had lost so much blood that the effort drained him. He collapsed beside me and I wasn't sure if he was alive or dead. The older man reached for the two discoloured dice in the water. He closed his fist over them.

'Are you really only sixteen inside that skin?' I asked him.

'I'm every age and no age,' he whispered. 'I'm dying and I'm scared. Give me your hand.'

His ancient hand looked feeble, criss-crossed by lines that no palmist could decipher. But if he was telling the truth, there was a boy four months older than me trapped within that skin. I reached out my good hand to clasp his. His grip was suddenly vice-like, as if he had been saving every last ounce of strength for this moment. I did not realise that he still had the black-handled knife until he nicked my palm and then cut open his own wrist. Dropping the knife, he pressed the dice into my clenched fist and held it tight as our blood mingled.

'No!' I cried. 'You won't use me to live! Go down to hell!'

The younger figure scrambled weakly towards us. At first I thought that he was trying to free my hand. Then I saw the same desperate determination in his eyes. He wanted to push the old man aside and take his place. His blood from the stab wound mingled with my blood. Both lay on top of me, trying to plunge down my fist that held the cursed dice into the water. The well looked only a few feet deep, yet I knew that it went down for ever. I knew that if I tumbled into it they would fall down after me and the stones would give way, and all three of us would plunge to our deaths. Their faces had a similar look.

'Let go!' they shrieked, 'let go!' I could not tell if they were addressing me or each other. Then the dice came loose from my grasp. I tried to hold on but I couldn't. As the dice spun towards the water I heard them shout with one voice, 'I want it back!'

All three of us fell forward. As my head plunged into the water, I realised that there were faces waiting for me in the well. I could see the face of my father and both my grandmothers, alongside a host of other faces who meant nothing to me. But I meant something to them. They were my blood ancestors, summoned by my father; they were the protective faces who had pressed against the windows of that stolen car on Bull Island. They surrounded me as icy water filled my nostrils, their love seeming to hold me safe while that shout reverberated inside my brain: I want it back.

I could still hear Shane and Thomas screaming those words, but another voice was drowning them out. It was my own voice, shouting the same fervent wish. I closed my eyes because my father was whispering not to look at the long procession of beseeching faces slowly being sucked out from the mouths of Shane and Thomas – each face inside a separate air bubble. These long-dead souls grabbed at my hair, clawed at my face, trying to cling onto me for life. Some had innocent faces and beseeching eyes; others had features contorted by evil. I could sense this chain of ghosts who had been living inside Shane's body and Thomas's body and Joseph's body before that. But I also sensed another line of ghosts whom my father had summoned to form a shield of protective love around me. And even amid my terror, I knew that my father's love was holding me tight and that he would not let go until all danger had passed.

I placed my trust in him as I continued plunging down through the water. I had no idea how deep the well was or how many ghostly fingers kept trying to pull me in amongst the great whirlpool of the dead that surged around me, the Blackrock ghosts released through the mouths of Shane and Thomas. But I could sense them starting to fight amongst themselves. Some souls were struggling to break free and face the judgement or oblivion that lay ahead. Others continued to plead to me: Open your mouth and let us enter. We will live in your vein; we will pulse in your blood; we will teach you to live for ever.

I knew I had to make a choice, that Shane and Thomas were offering me the chance to enter a limbo where I would never need to confront death. I could live on inside their chain of souls and be immortal. But if I refused to accept my own death, then how could I ever experience my life? I needed death to make sense of my life, to give it a beginning and an end. I didn't wish to live forever, because that meant not to truly live at all. Allowing myself to drown in this well would be my last conscious act, and therefore, I chose to live it fully. With my eyes tightly closed, I yielded myself up to death.

I felt Shane's and Thomas's fingers clawing at me one last time but the ghosts of my ancestors held me protected within their linked hands. My father's voice spoke: *I was weak and imperfect, son; no mortal soul is ever perfect. You cannot write the perfect song or live the perfect life. Don't waste your life chasing immortality. Don't live in anyone's shadow. Just know that I love you. Live every day to the full during your single precious stab at life.*

Then the sensation of drowning stopped. It was replaced by a sense of hurtling backwards at speed, as if life was being rewound like the spools of some great master tape. Shane and Thomas were still screaming, but their voices kept drifting further away. I had no idea where they were going – heaven or hell or oblivion or limbo – and no idea of what I should expect when I opened my eyes. Then the speeded-up sensation of movement stopped and I knew that my father was about to speak for one last time. I knew also that somehow I had been granted my wish by his love, which had helped me not succumb to a chain of evil. I had got it back – the most precious gift: I had been granted back possession of my life.

Epilogue

Joey

I had no notion of what lay ahead on the night that I accepted my death, the night I stopped falling through the freezing water, the night when that sense of hurtling backwards through time halted and my father's voice whispered for one last time, It is now safe to open your eyes. His voice was distant, as if he had been watching over me for years but was finally ready to move on to wherever it is that the dead go. My eyelids became infused with such bright morning light that, for a moment, it hurt to open them. Instead I reached out blindly and felt my fingers touch the polished wood of a classroom door.

I knew, then, where I was and what I had got back. I pushed open the door and entered a crowded classroom, crammed with faces that briefly turned to take in the new boy. Their glances were more dismissive than curious. There was no hostility in anyone's eyes. I was too ordinary to be of interest. But a girl with jet-black hair looked up and smiled for one second before looking away.

That smile was enough to give me strength, as it would often give me strength in the years to come. It would be some months before Geraldine grew relaxed enough to take my hand and open up her heart. On that evening – three months after my first day in Stradbrook College –

she brought me to see the Sion Hill duplex where, two years previously, her friend for a summer had died from smoke inhalation, having been found cradled in the arms of his father who rushed back in to try and save him. Geraldine confessed how she once thought she had been in love with Shane O'Driscoll, but only realised what love felt like when she met me.

That same evening, after passing the construction work going on where an old dairy used to stand on Castledawson Avenue, we walked on towards Booterstown to visit the tiny graveyard behind the Esso garage on the Merrion Road. A fresh tombstone there recorded how Thomas McCormack was finally united with his two brothers. Geraldine left flowers for the old man whom Shane and she had befriended during the summer when they played at being detectives – a man later found dead in the cellar of the house which he had left seventy years before to explore the world.

It would take five years before I recorded my debut album, *New Town Soul*. This contained six original tracks by me and six songs by my father, discovered on a tape in a teacher's attic. Was it a success? Was I famous? Reader, for the briefest time I was truly immortal, being played on every radio station. The problem with immortality, of course, is that it doesn't last for ever. Since then, I have known the ups and downs of any musician's life – heartbreak and joy, failure and unexpected successes. In short, I have enjoyed the miracle of a normal life, where I have tried to live every day as if it was uniquely precious and to appreciate this miracle about which I can tell nobody – the miracle of having wished for and having been given a second chance to live my life – a chance which I grasped on that morning when I glanced behind me in the classroom doorway to find that no other boy was standing at my shoulder. The chain of evil had been broken by the ghosts of my own ancestors whose love had formed a wall around me. But now those family ghosts were gone too. One day I may meet my father's spirit again in some other realm, but for now I knew that I was truly on my own as I walked through the chattering students to claim the empty desk by the window.

I wasn't nervous, and I did not pretend to look busy. I did not think about Shane or Thomas or that house on Castledawson Avenue. They seemed like figments from a bad dream. I did not try to make sense of the past; I simply accepted this gift of a fresh start. The sun was warm against the windows. I had been unhappy in my previous school, but a whole new life stretched ahead for me. This time I knew that I could only live it once, so this time I determined to grasp its every last ray of happiness.

Sitting quietly at the window desk, I waited for Geraldine to turn her head and smile.

Author's Note

New Town Soul was written while I was engaged in a residency in Blackrock as part of the Dún Laoghaire-Rathdown County Council 'Place & Identity Per Cent for Art Programme'. I would like to acknowledge the support of this programme and express my thanks to Ciara King, Carolyn Brown and the other staff of the Dún Laoghaire-Rathdown County Council Arts Office and the libraries and staff of the Dún Laoghaire-Rathdown County Council Library Service. I am also deeply grateful for the advice of Siobhán Parkinson and Elaina O'Neill of Little Island in Dublin, Derek Johns and Linda Shaughnessy of A P Watt in London and Beth Vesel in New York.

New Town Soul is inspired by my imaginative interpretation of the experience of life in Blackrock. It very deliberately plays with facts and aspects of its history. No resemblance is intended to any person, living or dead. While the streets where this book is set are real, no such house exists on Castledawson Avenue. But this is the role of the creative writer, to merge the real and the unreal, to show not just what exists in a place but what could exist, to insist that every young reader and young writer has the right to establish their own alternative, parallel imaginative space.

Dermot Bolger,
March 2010